THE LAST PERSON
IN THE WORLD

by Matthew Tree

Book design by vagabond

Instagram @vgbnd

Twitter @vgbnd

ISBN: 9798398211672

'Over the next few days I started to have flashbacks and began to feel emotions I'd not felt in years. Raw visceral fear. Intense shame. Burning anger.'

Anthony Daly, '*Playland*'.

PART ONE: POINTING A FINGER

I

I'd never have thought that me and Ralph Finns (his name at the time) would have got along well. Or at all. It's true that we were in the same year at our London-based public school, but I was a day boy from a lower-middle-class background who had scholarshipped his way into that otherwise unaffordable hive of affluent boys; and Ralph, a boarder, was the wealthiest of them all, so much so that he made the rest look practically insolvent (and me downright derelict) what with his Rolex watch, his state-of-the-art Bang & Olafsen sound system - on which he played Deep Purple and Blue Oyster Cult at full blast in his dorm room - his binging on vintage wines and his penchant for shoes so expensive that each pair – and he had not a few – would have kept a small African village in clover for a lustrum. And yet, to my surprise and possibly to his, we ended up becoming something a little less than friends and quite a bit more than acquaintances. Over the years, nodding terms became small talk became monthly, weekly, then (almost) daily conversations. I liked him because, despite his dour and sometimes sour demeanour and his probable inability to score more than two out of five in a empathy test – should such a thing have existed – he was not at all like a lot of the other boys at that particular seat of learning, most of whom, as it turned out, were obnoxious, self-assurance-oozing, top-hole

2

arseholes, every last monied mother's son of them. If I have to be honest.

When I asked him why he blew so much dough on himself, an admirably candid answer came out of that slightly puffy, inexpressive face of his:

"I'm taking everything I can now because maybe in the future I won't be able to have it."

He turned out to be right about that.

(His Dad had run a scrap metal business during the war years, selling tons of the stuff to a government that desperately needed it; if the man wasn't a multi-millionaire, he couldn't have been more than a few thousand quid off; his name popped up in the papers occasionally, belonging as he did to the outermost fringe of the great and the good).

Rolling in it though Ralph might have been, feckless he wasn't, being a dab hand with electronic devices of all kinds: he ∏could build radios, fix speakers, and was the go-to student for setting up the lighting for the school's theatre productions. Skills which turned out to be very handy in his future line of business. Essential, even.

As for me, I was trying to live up to my parents' expectations by doing well enough in my exams to get into university. Meanwhile, in my spare time, I was getting interested in the Real Workers' Party, an extra-parliamentary, more-or-less-Trotskyist faction. I even went to a couple of its rallies, which

3

made me feel I was doing something to make up for the privileged pigeonhole my scholarship had slotted me into.

*

One day, as we sat in the quad one afternoon, under grey sunlight, we got talking, Ralph and I, about our futures, just days before the end of school. It turned out that Ralph wasn't going on to a university like myself, but then again I assumed he didn't need to because he probably had a well-paid, gift-wrapped position in some big company, all ready and waiting. When I asked him what his future held in store for him he shrugged and said:

"My old man's got a summer residence in Dorset. I'm going to hang out there for a while. It's pretty cool, as mansions go."

Rich though I knew his family to be, I was impressed.

"A *mansion?*"

"I'll be there for the next couple of months. Why don't you drop in some time? Got a pen and paper?"

Clouds Manor, Bincombe, West Dorset.

"Turn up whenever's convenient, no need to call first."

Then he waved at the school buildings around us, and, quite out of the blue, declaimed:

"You know what this place's function is and always will be? No more nor less than to groom its pupils for eventual inclusion in the upper ranks of the judiciary, the banks, the Civil Service, the three main political parties, the stock exchange, the country's biggest corporations and – for the more creatively minded or simply restless souls among them – the media. All those people we've been studying with, they're slated to be the country's future movers and shakers: carbon copies, as it were, of the people currently pulling the strings. Together with other schools of its ilk, our 'public school' – a term, by the way, which should be banned under the Trade Descriptions Act – forms part of an immense societal scam. A fix that's permanently in. And that's just the tip of a very nasty iceberg."

I was astonished. Never before had I heard him speak with such vehemence. Never before, for that matter, had I heard him say anything political and much less in this clear, concise way that, by contrast, made the speakers at the two rallies I'd attended sound hackneyed and robotic.

"I couldn't agree with you more, but I mean, aren't you a candidate for being a bit of a future carbon copy yourself?"

"No. And neither are you."

Never before, had he spoken to me in such a sincere, personal tone.

"How do you know? I haven't got a clue as to what I'm going to do after uni. For all you know, I might end up as just another stockbroker. Or managing director. Or TV producer."

"I doubt it. We've got more in common than you might think."

I wondered how he'd come to that conclusion. I had also started to wonder about his tip-of-the-nasty-iceberg comment. What did he mean by *that*? He eased his bottom off the low wall we were sharing.

"I gotta go. Like I said, swing by the mansion when you feel like it. But don't leave it much longer than a couple of months, 'cos after that I'll be moving on."

"Anywhere in particular?"

I was guessing Gstaad or Biarritz or Nice or Marbella.

"No. Just *on*."

*

I felt like it sooner than I thought. At a loose end once school was over and done with, I went to more RWP lectures, at which various books were recommended to the audience: Marx, Engels, Lukács, and Trotsky (it goes without saying) so I got hold of those and ploughed my way through a few of them. I had two months to kill before I started university, and this was the best death blow I could come up with. The more I read, the more I thought about Ralph's revealing speech that day in the quad. By the time my last pre-university week rolled around, I'd spent most of my time in my parents' flat and they were hinting that I should show some gumption. (Sometimes it surprised me that after all these years, they hadn't observed that gumption, together with its cousins acumen, resolve, initiative and drive, was simply not in my make-up: that my temperament, for better or worse, was, in general, bereft of oomph).

Ralph's standing invitation was as good an excuse as any to get away from home for a couple of days. Besides, I was curious to see what Ralph – having made it clear that he had some militant ideas of his own – would make of the ones I'd picked up from my recent reading.

*

I caught a train to Dorchester, and a bus from there to Bincombe, from where I walked to Clouds Manor, or rather to within sprinting distance of it, because when it hove into sight I stopped in my tracks, took a deep breath, and gawped: it had as many wings as a brace of grouse. Once I'd passed through the iron gates I found myself walking up a gravel drive that led, after a while, to a front door.

When I was barely a yard away from the entrance, Ralph appeared in it, grinning.

"Smile, you're on candid camera!"

He pointed up. Two closed-circuit TV cameras were leering from the eaves. Ralph stood aside to let me pass.

"Can't be too careful, what with all the stuff my folks have got in here."

The place smelt of leather, waxed wood, and old dog.

"Let's go to the drawing room. We've got the run of the house, by the way: Mum and Dad are on a holiday break in Tuscany."

"No brothers or sisters around?"

"I'm an only child."

His parents certainly did have plenty of 'stuff'. I spotted a couple of Canalettos, a Stubbs and a Hockney on the walls we passed. Some of the knick-knacks on the tables and in the display cupboards looked pretty valuable too. Once we had ensconced ourselves in the drawing room, which gave onto a garden large enough to be public, a dark-haired woman in her twenties came in and asked Ralph if we needed anything. She wasn't dressed as a maid: no black dress or white pinafore or lace headpiece, just jeans and a check shirt. She didn't sound like a maid, either, and he didn't sound as if he were addressing one.

"Hi, Sarah. If you could bring over a jug of Pimm's that'd be great."

"One Pimm's, coming up!"

She smiled and left. For some reason, I felt the need to whisper.

"Is that the –?"

"That's the butler. Mum and Dad didn't want a stiff-necked man in funereal get-up, they preferred someone informal but efficient. And she's as competent as they get."

As indeed she proved by bringing the Pimm's, garnished with mint and cucumber, just minutes later.

"There you go, Ralph", she said, "as you've got a guest, I made up a Royal Cup."

"Wow, that's perfect, Sarah. Many thanks."

And she was off again.

"I'm obviously not very well up on the ways of the other half, Ralph. What's a Royal –?"

"Pimm's topped up with champagne," Ralph said, pouring some of the stuff into a glass for me. "Beats mother's milk into a cocked hat."

I sipped, several times, and started to relax.

"This being my first time in a mansion," I said, "Can I ask if Sarah is the only servant or do you have –?"

"Dear God, no. There's a cook, two cleaning ladies, a team of gardeners and a handyman to service the central heating and whatnot. But Sarah's the only live-in retainer. The others come in from Bincombe or Dorchester. They're on a rota."

I found myself whispering again.

"Sarah's kind of attractive. Have you ever –?"

He cut me short, a touch severely.

"No way! She's twenty-six. We nineteen-year-olds don't interest her."

We nineteen-year-olds drank some more Pimm's. I mentioned I'd been getting more or less involved with the RWP, and reeled off a list of the authors I'd been discovering. Ralph made a dismissive gesture with his hand.

"Politics", he proclaimed, "is crap."

Taken aback, I muttered:

"But you certainly had some ideas of your own about that school we've just been released from. All that stuff you said about people being slated for success or 'success', and carbon copies and so on. 'An immense societal scam': your exact words. Sounded pretty political to me."

He shook his head so vehemently that his silky brown hair flopped over half his face. Once he'd swept it back into place, he said:

"That was and is common sense, pure and simple. I mean, look where I come from," he gestured at the drawing room by way of indicating the entire country house, "I know exactly how the so-called Establishment works. I've grown up in it. And as far as I'm concerned, political parties like the one you seem to be getting involved in are never going to change anything. They're flogging a dead horse. Pissing in the wind. Labouring under a delusion. Whatever. No offence meant."

"None taken," I replied, dishonestly. No sooner had he finished talking than a phone rang somewhere in the house. Then stopped. Sarah called out:

"Ralph! It's for you."

He got up.

"Excuse me a minute."

"Sure."

But it wasn't a minute. When ten had gone by, I got tired of waiting about and strolled around the room, then out of it. I stopped by a door that was ajar, opened it and found myself peeking into a well-stocked library. I went in, curious to see what the really well-heeled read. There was an entire wall devoted to first-edition hardbacks of modern thrillers and detective stories by well-known writers in the genre. Another section held biographies of or autobiographies by significant British politicians, going back to Neville Chamberlain. There was also a Folio Society collection of classics – Dickens, Hardy, Austen, Trollope, Conrad and all the rest of them – that looked pretty much untouched. Then my eye ceased to rove, because not far from the classics, there were several shelves full of left-wing literature. Not just Marxist writing – although there was plenty of that too, some of which I was more or less familiar with by now – but also Bakunin, along with Kropotkin, Proudhon,

Godwin, Stirner, Rocker, Malatesta, Goldman, Bookchin and Chomsky. And Debord and Vaneigem and Jorn. I plucked out a copy of *The Society of the Spectacle*; it was well-thumbed. I removed Bookchin's *Post-Scarcity Anarchism*, gave it a quick flick-through, and found certain passages had been underlined. I tried Marcuse's *Counterrevolution and Revolt* and was surprised to find copious notes in the margins and even more surprised when I recognised the handwriting.

Then I heard Ralph calling my name.

"Where've you got to?"

I went out of the library and saw Ralph just as I was wandering along the corridor with all the nonchalance I could muster.

"Sorry to keep you waiting," he said, "something came up."

*

I spent two more days at Cloud Manor. We limited our conversations to minor mutual interests such as Led Zeppelin and brands of bitter, though there were times at the local pub, or during one long country walk, when I could barely refrain from asking him about all those well-thumbed radical titles in the library. I was pretty sure that his parents' reading material was limited to the thrillers, detective stories and the political biographies; and that Ralph was the only person in the place who could have bought and read Gramsci, Kropotkin and company.

*

The way Ralph and Sarah talked amongst themselves surprised me more and more. They would josh each other, occasionally with the odd expletive.

"Hop to it, Sarah, you slacker."

"You watch your mouth, little Lord Muck."

"No, seriously, you're a bit slow on the uptake today."

"Like fuck I am, your honour."

All said with tongues in cheek.

"You two seem to get on well together, for a master and servant."

He shrugged.

"Oh, Sarah's been here for years. She was hired back when my first pubic hairs appeared. And I was an early starter."

On day two, as we lounged about on big leather armchairs in the drawing room, a mite bored, he asked me if I'd like to go hunting. I'd never hunted a thing in my life. Indeed, I'd more or less forgotten there were still people who did.

"Hunting! Hunting *what*, for God's sake?"

A touch of a smile.

"Anything that moves."

"What?"

"Just kidding. We could start with some target practise and take things from there. Up for it?"

Not really, but I didn't want to look chicken.

"Sure."

"Great. Let's choose our weapons."

He took me down to the basement level, past a huge kitchen, into a room with a metal door to which he had the key. When it swung open, I gasped. Inside was a chamber of about thirty square metres, its back and side walls lined with rifles on racks.

"They let you have *access* to all this stuff?"

"I've taken classes. It's my hobby. Dad's too."

He moved ahead of me over to the far wall, unhooked a single-barrel shotgun from its stand, and held it out to me.

"Try this for size. For a novice, this is probably your best bet. Finnish and light as a feather. Gentle recoil, too. A beautiful piece."

Gingerly, I took the thing, supporting the barrel with my left hand and closing my right hand around the space where the butt met the trigger guard.

"Is it loaded?"

"Fuck no."

He pointed to a metal chest sitting in one corner.

"All the ammo's in there. Now let's see…"

He looked around for a moment, then unhooked a gun that looked longer and heavier than mine.

"This is a Blaser twelve gauge. Thirty-inch barrel. My favourite."

He laid it on the floor, took out a second key and unlocked the chest. Lying on the top of its contents were two sleeveless hunting jackets. He handed one to me.

"Best to wear one of these. They've got useful pockets."

The next thing I knew, he was giving me a small box that rattled. I shucked on the jacket and put the box in one of the side pouches. Ralph slung his rifle over his arm, barrel downwards.

"I'll get some bottles."

*

We walked into the garden and along a long strip of lawn to a weather-worn wooden table. Ralph opened the plastic bag he'd been carrying and placed six empty wine bottles on the table, about half a foot apart. As we backed off to take pot-shots at them, I glanced at the dates on the labels. 1961. 1953. 1945.

"You must have enjoyed drinking those."

"Yep. Take the last one on the left."

I pointed at the vintage empty he'd indicated and got it on my fourth shot. I winced.

"They wouldn't have me in the army."

"Nonsense. That wasn't at all bad for a first try."

He shouldered his own gun. He fired both barrels – with barely a second's difference between shots – and shattered the first two bottles on the right. As he reloaded, a couple of magpies fluttered out of a nearby tree. He slammed the gun shut, pulled back the bolt, aimed high and sent the two of them flopping down to earth. His face smothered in satisfaction, he muttered:

"Gotcha."

I shook my head.

"Jesus, Ralph, you're a crack shot. I never realised."

"Practise makes perfect. And here I can get all the practise I need."

I looked, not happily, at where the two birds lay skewed, just a few yards away.

"You can't eat magpies, right?"

He laughed.

"You can't eat most of the things I shoot around here. Killing them's the thing."

That slightly puffy, inexpressive face of his had not moved a muscle.

II

Just under a week later, I went up – as they used to say – to Wellingford, one of England's three oldest universities, which was much like the other two, what with its ancient edifices, and draughty, bicycle infected streets, its hot-dog vans whose steam smelt of uncleaned swimming pools, its be-scarved and overcoated students who slouched along the pavements with their heads down and eyes ditto as if expecting to be punched any second. The only thing that distinguished Wellingford from the two other venerable institutions it was usually associated with was that unlike them, it was very close to London: less than twenty minutes by train.

As for me, I was at an even looser end than before thanks to both a torpor and a certain mental discomfort caused by the university itself: its buildings, to my eyes, had something creepy about them, as if in the interstices of their centuries-old brickwork there lurked an unpleasant presence, invisible as gas.

Realising that my social life was going to be on the threadbare side if I didn't plump for some extra-curricular activity, I made myself, albeit with some misgivings, a member of the university branch of the RWP.

I'd chosen to study English literature, with a vague idea that this would somehow complement my Marxist fare. However, bored and restless in the evenings, I started to gravitate towards the pubs in which students were welcome (in the other ones, we got slow service or the wrong change, or both). Back then it wasn't normal for pubs to have TV, but there was just one that did: The Bird In Hand, which was student friendly, but without being for students only. The telly aside, it was much like any other pub: the bar and walls cladded with artificially aged wood; whiffs of dregs and stranded tobacco smoke; new mirrors with old Coca Cola ads printed on the silvering.

I hadn't made any friends yet. During those first solitary days, I found myself repairing nightly to The Bird In Hand where I would down a quiet pint or two of Holsten, and then leave, feeling peckish, after I'd seen the Nine O'Clock News.

On evening three and pint two, the newsreader mentioned a place I knew. Bincombe. The talking head gave way to a façade I knew even better. Clouds Manor.

I stood up and went over to the bar. The barmaid looked up. Wistful flaxen hair, a roundish face, a bored expression. I pointed to the screen.

"Could you put the volume up a bit, please?"

The pub was all but empty. She shrugged.

"I don't see why not."

As I hurried back to my chair, the newsreader said:

"Police have placed Ralph Finns, the son of one of Britain's most successful industrialists, Jeffrey Finns, on their missing persons list."

Up came, to my astonishment, a colour shot of Ralph.

"…also missing is the family's retainer, Sarah Jane Olsen…"

A picture of the butleress was flashed up in black and white.

"…Mr Finns reported his son's disappearance to the police after several days spent trying to locate him on his own."

Footage of a thin-faced, middle-aged man was shown, with the manor in the background.

"My son didn't tell me he was going anywhere and neither did Ms Olsen. However, the police have assured me that there is no immediate cause for alarm, and I personally hope and believe that this matter will be cleared up in the very near future. Ralph, if you're watching, please get in touch as soon as possible. Your mother is extremely upset."

Ralph's Dad, I was surprised to hear, had a working-class London accent, very different from his son's upmarket tones.

the talking head came back

19

"A police spokesman has confirmed they are investigating all available leads…"

a balding man in police uniform addressed the camera from behind a desk

"Nothing was removed from the house, including the personal effects of Ms Olsen and Ralph Finns. We are following several lines of investigation."

the talking head again

"Mrs Finns was unavailable for comment. And now, in Cambodia, the Khmer Rouge…"

I stood up and headed to the bar. The barmaid took my jar.

"Funny business, ay?" she said, as she filled it up. She looked as if she was two or three years older than me, and had the offhand manner townspeople often used with students. I nodded at the screen.

"It was about a friend of mine."

She stopped being offhand. Her eyes widened.

"What, that millionaire bloke?"

"His son. The one in the photo."

"Wow," she said, putting the pint in front of me, "I've never met anyone who's met anyone who's been on the telly."

At first I assumed this was the kind of thing I could expect a naive and possibly poorly educated barmaid to say, but there was an ironic glint in her eyes. I took a sip.

"But that's the point, he *hasn't* been on the telly. He's gone missing."

She switched off the TV, took my money, gave me the change, shook her head.

"Not for long."

"I'm sorry?"

"It's obvious, isn't it? He and that servant have done a runner."

"A runner?"

"They've eloped."

"So how come they didn't take any of their stuff with them?"

She gave me a *duh* look.

"That would've made them easier to trace, wouldn't it? The police would've issued a description of their things and every hotel and B&B in the country would be keeping its eyes open. No, either they just want to get away with a few weeks of uninterrupted nooky or maybe it's more serious and they'll get married, probably somewhere abroad that's hard to find. Either way, they'll surface sooner or later, mark my words."

I thought about how Ralph had told me there was nothing between him and Sarah. Come to think of it, he'd stressed the point. Which would make sense if they'd wanted to keep their sneaking-off a secret.

"You might be onto something there."

A full pint glass had appeared in front of me.

"There you go."

"But I didn't order –"

"On the house."

"Oh, well, thank-you –"

"Beth."

Said Beth, smiling winningly.

III

The following morning, my first thought was that I was waking up in my own room in college but instead found myself next to Beth's breathing body in her shared house in a part of town I'd never been in before. I recalled drinking through to closing time, and her insinuating that she wouldn't mind me spending the night with her and me asking her if she'd like to come back to my room, before I remembered that the college porters didn't let strangers stay on the premises. So I ended up walking to her place, which was so far away I had to stop not once but twice to pee in some bushes; after I'd offered diffident hellos to a couple of the other residents of her shared house, who were sipping cans in the living-room (male twenty-somethings with long hair and earrings in both lobes) we went upstairs and made love – well, shagged really – for the second time in my life but definitely not in hers.

Beth woke up moments after I did and when we'd made it down to the kitchen after making love (which, this time round, felt like the right way of putting it) I expressed surprise that the others had already gone. Beth gave me a stare.

"They're at something called *work*, but as a student, you might not understand."

It was tennish.

"No need to be so sarcastic. Besides, *you're* still here."

"I clock on at eleven. The others all work at the same site. Seven a.m. start. And I think you can take a little sarcasm from me, all things considered."

Followed by a peck on the lips.

*

I headed back to my room under a wood-pigeon-grey sky with my brain blossoming happily as it remembered more and more details about the previous night. Then, my mind having replayed all that sex as well as the I-don't-know-how-many-pints I'd had on the house, I recalled the TV news item about Ralph, and at the first newsagent's I came upon, bought all the broadsheets plus the Daily Mirror. When I got back to my room I laid them out on the bed. It wasn't that I expected Ralph's face to be splashed over every front page, but the disappearance of a filthy rich person's son should have merited at least a couple of banner headlines. But what *was* splashed over the front pages and in some cases several others as well was something that had happened later last night and that I'd missed. As had Beth.

All the papers carried photos of three houses. The one given the most attention was a luxury estate in central London called Unicorn Court. A bomb had been placed in the foyer, when nobody was about. There were images of shattered mirrors, a devastated flower arrangement, a smoking Axminster. The other two houses were in Preston, Lancashire. One was a boys' hostel, Durham House, and the other an approved school for girls called Owlcroft. The Lancashire bombings had taken place a little earlier than the one in London and the MO had been the same in both cases: a fire alarm had been set off so that all the occupants had had to be evacuated; only when everyone was out on the pavement did a small explosive device – a pipe bomb, the papers said – go off in each building, causing minor damage: shattered windows, scorched walls. Nobody had been killed or injured. I could just about see the point of attacking the luxury estate, if the idea was to have a go at rich people, but even then it struck me as a silly thing to do. And as for bombing the hostel and the school, that struck me as being simply bizarre .

A previously unheard-of organisation calling itself The Vanguard had called the Royal Society for the Protection of Cruelty to Animals, of all people. Their message:

Why these particular targets? Ask their owners. They know. *Au revoir.*

The Vanguard.

Several professional pundits declared that Britain now had its very own version of an armed left-wing gang, like Action

Directe in France, the Red Army Faction in West Germany, or the Weather Underground in America.

Which was all very well, but it was Ralph I wanted to find out about, because I'd known him for years; he was a real, flesh and blood person to me, and these Vanguard people were just another headline, so I went on skimming through the pages and finally found that in two of the broadsheets there were photos of him and Sarah (the same ones that had been flashed up on the news last night) and a gnat-sized item about their disappearance. Some of the other papers carried equally tiny items about them, without photos; and one of the broadsheets and the Daily Mirror didn't mention them at all.

*

A few days later, The Vanguard reappeared. And for a few weeks after that, they were quite the running saga.

A week after the pipe bombings, they drove a car past the Essex home of Jim Johnson, the presenter of 'Jumping Jimbo', Britain's favourite children's TV show, and peppered his front door with a machine-gun. I'd grown up watching this man and his team showing me how to make toy yachts out of toilet rolls; organising massive collections of milk bottle tops or jam jar labels for designated charities; and doing a different dance each week, pulling funny faces as he went through the moves, this being the most popular spot on the programme, given that Johnson was over six-feet tall, skeletally skinny and highly agile for a man in his late forties. A couple of years ago he'd started up a children's club for his young viewers – 'Jimbo & Co.' – whose membership card afforded them discounts to a variety of pantomimes, concert halls, bookshops and swimming pools; by the time of the drive-by, it had 400,000 members, aged between three and fourteen, for which feat Johnson had been knighted.

When I mentioned it at the pub that evening Beth shook her locks:

"Saw the news on the telly. I never liked Jumping Jimbo very much, I thought all that dancing about he did was kind of creepy. Having said which, shooting his door down is just plain daft."

My thoughts exactly. This time the responsibility note was even briefer than the first:

Just getting into our stride.

The Vanguard.

Like that, with the 'the' in italics.

*

Two days later, they gave the same treatment to the Kent home of Sebastian Hayley, a television chef whose trademark was preparing dishes from everywhere except England and – polyglot that he was – giving the foreign names as well as the English ones for all the ingredients. He wore a Savile Row suit while he poured and fried and boiled and sprinkled and plated and served. Sired by a family of considerable means, his accent was only a notch below that of the aristocracy. Like Johnson, the British citizens who hadn't heard of him could have been counted on two hands. Minutes after the second shooting a hand-delivered note was popped into the letterbox at the RSPCA's head office in Southwater:

We'll never let you spoil the broth again. Tootle pip, old chap.

The Vanguard.

Again, there seemed to be no clear motive. A police spokesman made a short statement on the Nine O'Clock News to the effect that 'investigations into the terrorist organisation that calls itself The Vanguard are continuing', his over-solemn face hinting that Scotland Yard didn't yet have a clue as to who or where The Vanguard was.

The third attack took place the following week. Members of this so-called Vanguard machine-gunned the home of Hugh Lowell, MP, in a working-class district of Preston.

Lowell had become famous for defending authentic dialect words – 'mack' for make and 'tack' for take and 'er' for she and 'owd' for old and 'mon' for man and so on – by speaking them loudly and clearly in public whenever he could. That, plus his down-to-earth irony and a smile which was considered cheeky, had endeared him to large swathes of the population as well as the media, which gave him plenty of air time and column space. The bullets left his front windows smashed to smithereens and his front door looking like a Swiss cheese. The message from the Vanguard?

You got nothing like your just desserts. Give us time.

Beth shook her head.

"The man's a working-class hero, for fuck's sake. What a bunch of nutters."

Indeed, there seemed to be neither rhyme nor reason to their actions. And the papers had made it repeatedly clear that they were as baffled as anyone else, with headlines like:

THE VANGUARD: THE LOONY LEFT, OR JUST PLAIN LOONY?

Not long after that, The Vanguard stopped performing: no more actions, no more communiqués. For the time being.

*

Ralph's disappearance, of course, was still on my mind, but was now slowly shifting onto a back burner, given that I was falling in love. Beth turned out to be a continuous source of surprises. Her favourite writers – and I confess, I was surprised she had any – were Franz Kafka, Elias Canetti and Virginia Woolf, all of whom I personally found hard going. She didn't have any A levels and had never crossed the threshold of a university building, but had an interest in the cultivation of her own brain which, as well as books, took in cinema, the occasional exhibition and plenty of music.

In bed, she broke me into oral sex and a couple of positions I'd previously been unaware of. And we joked about trying anal sex, without trying it. In fact, every day spent with Beth was like watching a window opening wider and wider on the, for me, sorely neglected real world.

I spent less and less time in the university, and more and more of it in Beth's bedroom or the pub where she worked. I stopped going to lectures, and limited myself to doing my obligatory weekly essay. But that was something close to a pleasure, given that I had taken a liking to my tutor, Alan Curtis, a solemn man who was close to being elderly; he was quiet and kindly, and indulgent with my not always good and sometimes downright sloppy essays on Wordsworth or Coleridge or whoever it was that week – and whose study's thick green curtains were kept fully drawn throughout the day. He had a penchant for dark brown suits and black lace-up Oxfords, which I noticed because they were like the ones my grandfather used to wear.

Though I dropped in on the university-based RWP meetings from time to time, I was finding them less and less interesting, consisting as they did of student party members repeating Marxist-Leninist dogmas, using slightly different wording in order to give the impression they weren't all running exactly the same tape. However, at one of these meetings an upcoming series of evening lectures from a London-based party 'organic intellectual' was announced. He would be coming up every Thursday to give a one hour talk on topical matters, that day's chair explained.

"And look," he said, pushing up his glasses and mumbling into his beard, "I know that some people don't find this caucus exactly electrifying," and he essayed the slimmest of smiles at the ten or so people around him, "but James Delaney is really worth a listen to. We've taken the risk of booking the

Matthew Arnold auditorium for him, as we think he'll attract quite a crowd."

*

The Matthew Arnold auditorium was a fifty-seater that had twenty people sitting in it when Thursday rolled around. There was no table and no chair, just a standing mike placed centre-stage.

The light dimmed, a shadow moved up onto the stage until a sudden spotlight revealed it to be a thin man with a bloated face, wearing a black shirt and jacket and black jeans and black boots that glimmered a touch. He could have been anywhere between thirty and forty.

"Good evening," he said, in a voice laced with a dash of Liverpudlian, "today I'd like to talk about racism. People often say there's always been racism and there always will be. This isn't true. Racism first reared its ugly head as recently as the late eighteenth century…"

Not having expected anything much other than the usual looped RWP fare, I sat straight in my seat, ears pricked up, delighted as Delaney took forty minutes to walk us through the origins of racism starting with pseudoscientific quotes from otherwise scientific luminaries such as Linnaeus, Kant and Herder, through to its acceptance as a supposedly proven reality in the nineteenth century, with consequences ranging from decades of lynching in the United States of America to the mass measurement of human heads in Europe. He explained how, in the case of the Jews, religious anti-Judaism was gradually replaced by racist anti-Semitism, thus slating all Jews for murder within the Nazi sphere of influence, irrespective of whether they had converted to Christianity or not. He ended with a list of racist incidents that had taken place in Britain within the last twelve months and explained how the discovery of the hominid Lucy just three years previously could be an indication that all humans originally came from Africa, something which would render the very concept of 'race' obsolete; a conclusion which elicited a gasp from his little audience.

My mind felt as cleansed as if it'd just stepped out of a bath and was now towelling itself down. Once he'd finished, he sat on the edge of the stage and a few of us went over to thank him. Last in line, I congratulated him with genuine enthusiasm and went as far as to say how refreshing it had been to listen to a left-wing speech that was free of cant.

"You're the first person who's pointed out that I deliberately avoid clichés."

He smiled. I felt, well, chuffed.

"Come back next Thursday," he said, "when I'll be putting the boot into religion."

IV

No sooner had I entered The Bird In Hand the day afterwards, at a quiet early hour, than Beth started brandishing a newspaper, and when I got to the bar she opened the centrefold, displaying her nice white teeth to me.

"Your mate," she said, "is in the Mirror." And so he was:

SON OF MILLIONAIRE INDUSTRIALIST CONFIRMS HE'S ALIVE AND WELL … AND HAPPILY MARRIED

Ralph and Sarah, arms around each other, were smiling seriously at the camera next to a splurge of tropical vegetation. In the background, a grainy row of palm trees could be made out.

"Christ," I said, "you were right about them eloping."

"Don't look so surprised."

"I'm sorry."

"No need to apologise."

'At 11.15pm last night, newly-weds Ralph Finns and former womanservant Sarah Jane Olsen informed Mr Finn's father, industrialist Jeffrey Finns, that they had married at an undisclosed location to avoid publicity and were planning a round-the-world trip by way of a honeymoon.

Ralph Finns stressed that he wished, above all, to ask forgiveness for the anguish that his disappearance had caused his parents.'

I moved on to the facing page, where Ralph's Dad had been given a longer interview, but a smaller photograph.

'Scrap metal mogul Jeffrey Finns told the Mirror: "After all he'd put his mother and me through, I confess I was angry when Ralph finally got in touch, but then on second thoughts, I felt so relieved that he was alive and well, I decided to cut him some slack." This 'slack', he revealed, is enough cash to allow Ralph and his mint-condition spouse to celebrate their clandestine contract with a months-long honeymoon. "Extravagant?" mused Mr Finns, "I suppose it is. But afterwards, Ralph's going to have to face up to the fact that it's time to knuckle down and get a job." As for his son's whereabouts, the man who made millions from any old iron shook his head. "Ralph doesn't want his honeymoon to be turned into a documentary," he said, "and that seems fair enough to us, all things considered. Having said which, I would like to take this opportunity to offer my most sincere apologies to the police for the inconvenience caused by the irresponsible behaviour of my son and his fiancée."

Mrs Finns was unavailable for comment.'

Beth snorted.

"They can apologise all they want, but it just goes to show that if your family's got stacks of money, you can get away with anything. If I'd pulled a stunt like that, they'd have locked me up and made me pay for the cost of the search."

She pointed at the photo of Ralph and Sarah.

"I wonder where that was taken? Bali? Hawaii? The Seychelles?"

"They'll probably go to all those places and more. Some people have all the luck."

She gave me a sarcastic smile.

"Marxist, aren't you? I thought you lot wanted everybody to live in communal apartment blocks with shared toilets and porters working for the KGB."

I blushed.

"No, my lot, as you put it, want *everyone* to be able to enjoy places like… like Bali, not just a privileged few."

She touched my arm.

"Sure you do. Now if you'll excuse me, I've got some lumpen proletarians to attend to."

I turned to the door at which she'd just nodded. A bunch of hooray-henry type students had irrupted into the saloon bar, their voices plummy, their laughs fake.

*

The next Thursday, I went back to the Matthew Arnold auditorium – now almost full – to listen to what James Delaney had to say about religion. The *mise-en-scène* was the same: the single spotlight, the black clothes.

"Religion has existed for a longer period of time than racism, but like racism, it hasn't always been with us. For thousands of years, people's lack of scientific information about the world led them to indulge in magical thinking. What we today call superstition…"

He went on to trace the emergence of priest-kings from what he called 'the primeval ooze of sorcery', and about how the rise of agriculture brought about the formation of towns and cities, followed by the quasi-separation of the priestly and political functions, with royalty enjoying its divine right and ecclesiastics acquiring political clout; a separation that finally gave rise to the organised religions and extant monarchies we know today. He also showed how easy it was to start up a religion, citing Mormonism, the cargo cults and Raëlism as recent examples; as a finale, he explained why religious belief, when exacerbated, can lead to excessive and often violent behaviour.

It was a tour de force of a talk, better even than the last one and just as jargon-free. This time round, I was one of the first to congratulate him. He smiled.

"You were here last week, right?"

"And I'll be here next week as well."

He hesitated, as if a thought had struck him:

"How long have you been with the RWP?"

"About four months."

"And are you keeping the faith?"

"I'm sorry?"

"No doubts at all?"

"Well, now that you ask… I do have some, yes."

His expression sat up.

"Listen," he said, "what are you doing after this?"

I'd arranged to see Beth, but later on.

"Nothing much."

"Fancy a coffee?"

*

"So what do you think could be done to make the RWP more effective?" he asked, stirring his white coffee in the working-class café he'd taken me to. I put down my cup of tea, not having expected a leading party official to ask this of me.

"I don't know," I said, "but getting together twice a month to comfort each other with quotes from Marxist scripture isn't going to change much."

He laughed, a little bit.

"What about the demos? We get a pretty big turnout, as you know."

"Whenever I've been on a demo, afterwards I've always felt I've been let down. Demos always make me feel, well, I don't know if I should say this…"

"Say it anyway."

"Post-coital."

A chuckle.

"So, what would you propose?"

"I don't know. But something more…"

"Attention-catching?"

"Maybe."

"Which college are you at?"

I told him. It took him a single gulp to finish his coffee.

"Nice talking to you."

He got up and left.

V

Beth had the evening off, and we'd decided we'd hole up in her room with some fish and chips, a six pack of lager and a bottle of white wine. I'd got the booze, and she the fish.

After a mutual hand job, we snuggled down in front of her small black and white set, waiting (with the sound off) for *The Day of the Jackal* to come on, drinking the beers first, keeping the wine on hold, picking at the chips before even thinking of laying our hands on the cod.

On her single bookshelf there were now nearly a dozen or so volumes (the ones I'd already seen – Kafka, Canetti and Woolf – plus a couple of volumes of Victorian porn and Simone de Beauvoir's *The Second Sex*). I noticed a couple of drawings had been blu-tacked to her light grey walls: charcoal renderings of two faceless, genital-less couples embracing each other passionately.

"What are those?"

She blushed a touch.

"I go to the odd evening class when I get the chance. Painting and drawing."

I pointed to the pictures.

"They're good."

She poked me in the ribs, half-pleased, half-sarky.

"An expert, are you?"

"No, but as an aunt of mine says, I know what I like."

It was good to see her smile and as my second beer settled down inside me I felt a comfort that hovered, stable, in the air. Beth smelt of shampoo and a dash of supermarket perfume and I realised there and then that this was the best combination possible, the only combination desirable: soap and shop brand scent; and that this was the only place I wanted to be, the only place I needed to be, that all was well with the world inside her room, the telly muted and the chips tentatively tasted, the drawings on the wall, and her and I taking swigs from cans that were still chilled, even as beyond the walls of her room the rest of the world swarmed and glowered, crept and lurked, its eyes untrustworthy, its limbs rustling sneakily through the night. Let things stay like this, I said to myself, just like this, exactly like this, just us and the beer and the take-away and the flickering black and white motion on the screen.

I smiled. She looked at me.

"Happy?"

"Happy."

"Maybe we should try the cod."

As we did so, the news came up.

"Want to see this?"

I shrugged.

"Why not?"

Another murder by the Yorkshire Ripper. A spat between the National Front and anti-Nazi protesters, including some from the RWP.

"Shouldn't you have been in that?"

I sighed.

"I suppose I should. But I wasn't, was I?"

She pointed to the melee of skinheads giving the Hitler salute to the protesters, with police trying to form a line between the two groups.

"I'm glad you weren't."

As we wolfed down the fish, a caption popped up:

POLICE REPORT NO FURTHER LEADS IN VANGUARD
INVESTIGATION

Followed by a brief clip of a police spokeswoman reporting there were no further leads in the Vanguard investigation.

"That bunch of idiots," Beth said, "have been quiet since those shootings. Just as well. If you start messing about with bombs and guns, in the end someone's going to get badly hurt."

"But they haven't been so far," I said, surprised by my surprise.

"Don't tell me you're in favour of those people?"

Alarm in her voice, lined with anger.

"No! You know what my politics are."

"Yeah. Why don't you open the wine?"

As it began its slow journey through our veins, *The Day of the Jackal* came on. We watched Edward Fox go through his deadpan paces for half an hour before we started kissing then petting then making love and it was when we were in full coitus that the bang went off, a bang so loud it made the windows shudder and my penis fly out of its burrow. We sat up simultaneously.

"What the fuck was that?"

"I've no idea. It wasn't a car backfiring, that's for sure."

Beth started redressing in a hurry.

"Let's take a look."

We trotted down the stairs to a front door already opened by the other tenants, of whom there were a total of four, I now saw, one of them with snaky tattoos on both arms. They were pointing at a flickering glare just visible somewhere beyond the rooves of the houses opposite.

The tattooed one turned to Beth. "We were thinking about taking a look-see. Want to come?" He glanced at me. "You too, if you want."

"Sure," said Beth. The others were already opening the doors of a shabby-looking Ford Cortina. The tattooed man was at the wheel. I squeezed into the back and sat on Beth's lap. We headed in the general direction of the glare and when we were close enough to feel heat blowing our way, the man in the front passenger seat said:

"I think it's Saint Martin's."

Barely had he got the words out of his mouth than we were flagged down by two policemen in yellow fluorescent jackets.

"No vehicles beyond this point."

We parked, got out and walked past a half dozen semi-Ds to a cordon beyond which, sure enough, a parish church was burning. High flames rose out of its now vanished roof, spiralling into the night, their tips releasing strings of black smoke. Dozens of spectators, their bellies pressed against the police tape, were gazing, staring, gawping at the blaze. Beth had a hand over her mouth.

"Stupid bastards!"

The tattooed man turned to her:

"You know who did this?"

She took her hand away.

"I can bloody well guess."

*

Back at the house, we tuned into a news channel on the radio. A male voice was saying, hurriedly:

"…parish churches in Nottingham and Wellingford were bombed simultaneously at eleven forty-five tonight. Responsibility has already been claimed by the terrorist organisation that calls itself…"

Beth looked at me.

"Told you!"

"A message phoned through to *Vogue* magazine said the following: 'God's servants are not to be trusted. The Vanguard.' Nobody was injured in the attacks, but in Wellingford, the roof of Saint Martin's Parish Church was completely destroyed and the inner walls severely scorched…"

Footage.

"…on the other hand Saint Peter's Church in Nottingham was barely scathed, with minimal damage done to the foot of an altarpiece."

Footage. Beth shook her head.

"They're fucking certifiable."

"But, like I said, they still haven't hurt anybody."

The four men and Beth looked at me. I thought they were about to say something. But no.

VI

I slept so late I was the only person in the house when I opened the front door and stepped into the midday chill. I did the longish walk back to my college, hands in pockets, thoughts drifting hither and thither: the first third of *The Day of the Jackal*; being on top of Beth; the flames flowing upwards from the church…

I passed under the college arch, watched ostentatiously by the porter.

"Morning, absentee!"

He was a permanently bad-tempered man who I suspected was a cashiered copper. I headed for my room, in which I'd left three course books strewn about, one open, two closed. I was staring at them blankly when there was a sharp knock on the door.

The only person who ever knocked on my door was the college scout, a harried looking Maltese whose job was to empty the students' wastepaper baskets, as if we were incapable of carrying out that specific task ourselves. I opened the door, expecting to see a small man in a white jacket, but instead I got a black jacket, black shirt, and black jeans tucked into black boots.

"May I come in for a moment?"

I stood instantly to one side to allow James Delaney to stride past me.

"It's a bit of a mess," I said.

"Of course it is," he said, "you're a student. Can I sit down?"

"Please!"

He took one of the two armchairs and I sat down in the other. Only now did I ask myself how he'd got past the porter, who took his job of turning unauthorised visitors away very seriously. I would have asked Delaney if he hadn't spoken first.

"I hope you don't mind me coming by for another little chat." Without giving me time even to show any polite acquiescence, he went on: "The last time we spoke, I got the impression that you don't think the RWP is going to make a real difference, let alone initiate a revolution. So might I ask why you're with them?"

Thrown off balance, I came up with something that sounded pat enough to have been spouted in a caucus get-together:

"I suppose I wanted to do something, *anything*, that would help undermine the status quo."

At that, he humphed.

"Which begs the question, what's wrong with the status quo?"

For that I had an answer of my own, albeit partly plagiarised from Ralph's radical speech, the one that'd so pleasantly surprised me.

"I was taught to do my utmost to do well, to get into a good school, to get into a good university like the one we're sitting in, and all I've seen so far is that the whole system is rigged, rigged from top to bottom, you're inserted into it at one level or another and once you're in you have to do your best with your allotted lot. If you're a miner, you stay a miner. If you're a university graduate, you're most likely on the fast track to a pot of gold. I've seen how very early on – school, university – they mark the cards and load the dice. What's wrong with the status quo, you ask? What's *right* with it?"

He was staring at me. Quiet as mice, he said:

"You talk about 'they'. Who are 'they'?"

I hesitated.

"Well, the people at the top, I suppose. And the companies and institutions they control or run."

"The people at the top…"

A thin smile.

"…and what would you do to these people, if you got half a chance?"

He leaned forward.

"You wouldn't, say, bomb their property? Or take pot shots at their front doors?"

"Like this Vanguard group have been doing?"

He nodded.

"Tell me, what do you make of that particular organisation?"

"I think they're off their rocker."

"How so?"

"Nothing they've done makes sense. Well, bombing a luxury estate, maybe, at least from a radical point of view. But an approved school? Or shooting up the home of a working-class politician? That's absurd."

"And what, in your opinion, wouldn't be absurd? If you could do anything you liked, what would you do?"

Another pat answer:

"I'd take power and money away from the people who've got most of both things, and use them more fairly."

No sooner had I said it, than I blushed.

"So," he said, brushing back a flock of dark hair, "you want to be *fair*."

He sat back, and concentrated for a minute on the backs of his hands. Then he was staring at me again.

"I could give you a chance to be fair. Very fair."

"I'm sorry?"

A pause. Another examination of his hands. Then his eyes honed in on mine.

"I'm going to take a risk and tell you something that cannot and must not be mentioned to anyone else. Not to your friends or family. Not to Beth."

My stomach twitched.

"How come you know about –?"

"Listen to what I have to say and everything will make perfect sense. I am, as you know, an active member of the RWP…"

A 'top official', I'd been told. Maybe he was on the Central Committee and all.

"…but I also have a day job…"

Yet one more wafer-thin smile.

"…working for the government."

He paused again, and looked at me as if he expected some sort of reaction.

"You're a civil servant?"

"After a fashion. I'm in security."

My eyes widened, of course.

"You're working for the *police?*"

"No."

As he seemed to be playing a guessing game, I guessed. Incredulously.

"MI5?"

"As it's popularly known."

I sat back, trying to get my head round this information. I knew that at the universities like the one I went to, the supposedly best ones, MI5 recruited on a basis as regular as it was casual. I'd heard stories about students being accosted in the street and asked straight out if they'd like to join. But I'd never have thought they'd accost me.

"But you said yourself you're an active member of the RWP!"

"Let's say that's a kind of hobby. The far left interests me. As it does my superiors, of course. But I haven't come here to talk about the RWP."

I frowned.

"Do you mean you're spying on us? If that's the case, what's to stop me telling my comrades?"

"You could do that, of course. Nothing to stop you. But there *would* be consequences. Regrettable ones."

For a moment, I wondered if this was some kind of practical joke. And he, some kind of weirdo.

"Is that a threat?"

"It's a fact. Listen, if you wish to terminate this conversation here and now, all you have to do is say so. I will go back to being – in Gramsci's words - an organic intellectual for the RWP, and you will go back to your studies. End of story. Either that, or we continue, although I warn you that if we do so, you will be privy to information far more compromising than that which I have just given you."

Did he know that I was no more interested in my studies than I was in, say, collecting traffic cones? Did he know that the only time that mattered to me was spent with a girl whose first name he somehow knew? And what, I asked my stultified nineteen-year-old self, was being dangled in front of me? What could be so 'compromising'?

What the hell.

"Fire away."

He crossed his legs and interwove the fingers of both hands.

"The Vanguard."

"What about it?"

"As you may be aware, the police are not having much luck with their enquiries."

"They don't seem to have any leads, that's for sure."

"They haven't got a bastard clue."

He leaned forward.

"But we have."

"I'm sorry?"

"We have a possible suspect. Given the efficiency and professionalism of the Vanguard's actions, we surmised that one of its members may – or perhaps must – have been in the military. We then came across a particular SAS man who deserted while on a two-year tour of duty in Northern Ireland. He wasn't showing any of the signs of combat fatigue that usually precede an AWOL. He was an explosives expert, one of the best in the field. He disappeared just over four months ago."

He breathed out, pinched his nose just above the bridge, and ran a hand back over his hair again. Only then did it occur to me that he might be a touch stressed.

"Look," he said, "I'm not one hundred per cent sure I should be telling you all this…"

Indeed, why was he?

"…but we do have a national security threat on our hands and our attitude is, frankly, any port in a storm. Normally we wouldn't approach someone who was so young and inexperienced. Do you mind if I smoke?"

He was asking *me?*

"No, please go ahead."

He reached into a jacket pocket, took out a flip-top packet of Silk Cut, lit up, sucked in, then released a whirl of bluish smoke. The cigarette trembled a little in his fingers.

"Of course I could try and approach this man myself, but he, being of a different political bent, wouldn't open up much to a high-ranking RWP official which is what, of course, he would take me for."

I was finding it harder and harder to digest his gist.

"So you know where he is?"

"We have a notion. The Army has something called a Deserter Information Point – just a phone number, really – that people can call if they spot anyone on French leave. Well, we got lucky. One of our man's former comrades in arms saw him in a pub. In this town."

I sat up.

"*Here?*"

"It's no coincidence that I organised a series of talks here, precisely. Of course, it would have been easy enough to hand matters over to the Army and let them pick him up…"

Another puff.

"…however, for various reasons, we didn't want the Army in on this one. I was told to set up a different kind of operation. And if you wish, if you feel up to it, if you think you've got what it takes, you can be a part of it."

Another exhaled spiral.

"Me? What could *I* do?"

"You've already done some of it. We tend to go by vectors. Vector one: you are one of the most regular of the regulars at the pub where our target was located."

"You mean –"

"The Bird In Hand. Vector number two: you are much the same age as the target. When you hit twenty next month, you *will* be the same age."

"But –"

He held up a hand.

"Vector number three: you're in the RWP but you're not satisfied with its methods, and independently of the party's tediously predictable Marxist line, you have a personal politics of your own. Got an ashtray?"

I ended up handing him an empty beer can:

"That's it, I'm afraid."

"That's fine."

He popped the butt into the can. It sizzled.

"Look, there are some things I just don't understand."

"Ask away."

"If you knew I was a regular at that pub, you must have hung around there yourself. But I never saw you."

"I have a couple of helpers. 'Assets', in the jargon. They alternated at the pub, looking for student regulars who were also in the RWP, or had been, using photos they'd previously committed to memory. There were exactly two candidates. Out of which, the most likely one was yourself."

I was more baffled than ever.

"The RWP? What's the RWP got to do with this?"

"The deserter was in it for a short while before he enlisted. Like you, he got fed up with the Marxist patois. And we suspect that he has, like yourself, a personal politics of his own."

"Now…"

He gripped my knee.

"...all I need is for you to keep on going to the same pub..."

He released my knee, reached into the inside pocket of his jacket and took out an envelope from which he extracted a black and white photograph of a uniformed man with a short back and sides encasing a clean-shaven face with worried-looking eyes.

"Take it please."

I did so, barely believing that this was happening.

"What's his name?"

"Frank Warner, the last time we looked, although he's almost certainly using an alias nowadays. If you see him in the pub, what I would like you to do is engage him in conversation, but only if the circumstances are propitious. For example, if you happen to find yourselves sitting side by side at the bar. After all, you do usually drink at the bar."

Beth.

"Remember that we don't know for sure that Warner is involved with the Vanguard. It's not much more than an educated guess. The trick is to kick off with some very small talk, to see if you can get some kind of rapport going. Enough, at least, to maybe get onto the subject of politics..."

Delaney stood up.

"...that's *all* we want, an attempt at a chat. If nothing comes of it, not to worry. This kind of thing has a habit of being a bit hit and miss."

Whoa, whoa, whoa.

"But wouldn't it be simpler for you just to arrest and interrogate him?"

Delaney shook his head.

"If he's the committed revolutionary we think he might be, he wouldn't give us anything, even under pressure. He *was* trained by the SAS, after all."

The SAS.

"Is he dangerous?"

"We don't think he'd do anything rash inside a hostelry or any other public place…."

Hostelry?

"…But just to be on the safe side, those assets I mentioned will be keeping an eye on you. And I repeat, please, not a word about this to anybody. Beth included, remember?"

Whoa, whoa, whoa. I had not said I was going to do this.

"I'm not sure if I'm the right person. I don't know if I've got what it takes, as you put it. In fact, I'm pretty sure I haven't. I'm afraid I'm going to have to say no. I'm sorry."

He leaned forward.

"You should have told me that back when I asked you if you wished to terminate the conversation, but you said to go ahead, so I did. I took that to mean you were ready and willing to do something for your country, which is why I have given you a not insignificant amount of classified information. If you back

57

down now, you not only compromise me, you compromise a top priority security operation. Do you know what compromising an on-going security operation of this importance is called?"

No.

"No."

"It's called treason. And even in this day and age, the penalty for treason is what it always has been. Have I made myself quite clear?"

Clear enough to make me realise then and there that if I wanted this increasingly scary man to leave, there was nothing else I could or rather *should* do but nod and say yes.

"Yes."

"I'm glad to hear it. After all, we're not asking for the moon. Just an attempt at a little powwow, and even then, only if the opportunity arises. Compared to what many other people have done for this country, that's not such a big deal. Now is it?"

I shook my head.

"No."

"Any further questions?"

"Let's say I do manage to talk to this person. How would I contact you afterwards?"

"You wouldn't. I'll be doing the contacting."

He stood up and held out his hand. I let mine be shaken.

"Good luck," he said as he slipped out of the door, leaving me feeling as if I'd just been mugged.

VII

"You seem somewhat distracted this morning."

Professor Curtis looked at me over the top of his spectacles. I was in an armchair facing him and had just tried to answer a question of his about my essay on Dickens, and failed (it came out as a cough). In his habitual almost-whisper of a voice, he said:

"I'll repeat the question. I was interested in hearing why you wrote that Dickens's characters often appear to be hysterical."

Oh.

"That's because well over half of them are always exclaiming, or talking compulsively, or obsessing over something, or are in some kind of deep depression, or are having fits of unpredictable behaviour."

"And?"

"We usually think of the Victorian era as being very staid, very solemn, very formal, and, well, dull. But in Dickens you've got all these people yelling their heads off and jumping about and kicking up a fuss, which doesn't tally with the image we tend to have of that period."

Professor Curtis inhaled, sat back, and put a hand over his mouth. The seconds ticked by until so many had passed that I wondered if I should ask him if the tutorial was over. Just when I was about to do so, he muttered:

"I think that what Dickens was saying, with these volatile characters, is that there are people who might seem perfectly normal at first sight but that deep inside they have these urges and passions and desires and frustrations which they hide from prying eyes. Dickens, however, makes them wear their hidden impulses on their sleeves, turning his characters inside out, as it were, so that their inner selves are revealed for all to see."

He said the last four words with a pause between each, as if placing a full stop before them: For. All. To. See. He looked up, his face twisted in a grimace that didn't look intentional. He straightened it out in a flash.

"On which note, I believe we can call it a day."

*

As had been my wont for a while, that evening I went to The Bird In Hand, but this time I had the feeling I'd been shoved into a film whose script I hadn't been allowed to see.

I sat at the bar, got served my usual pint by Beth, and looked round the room several times over until I was convinced that Frank Warner wasn't present.

"And a good evening to you, too."

I hadn't so much as said hello.

"Hi, Beth. Bit distracted today."

She frowned.

"You OK? You look like a fart just followed through."

"Really? No, everything's fine. No poop in *my* pants."

I started a smile, but the sound of the door opening behind me put me on alert. A new customer approached the bar and ordered a pint of cider. I looked at him to see if he was the man in Delaney's photo. No. When he turned to look for a free table, Beth hissed at me:

"What the fuck's wrong with you? You were staring at that customer like you wanted to pick him up."

"I'm sorry, Beth. I just…"

"You just what?"

I had no wish to put Mr Delaney's threats to the test.

"It's just not my day."

To lower my tension, I drank more than my normal quota. No one dropped in who remotely resembled Delaney's deserter.

That night, at Beth's place, for the first time with her I was unable to get an erection and not for lack of her trying. Thankfully, she took this in her stride.

"It's not your night, either."

And she rolled over and went to sleep. I rolled over, and didn't.

*

As the week passed and Mr Warner continued not to put in an appearance, I began to relax a bit. After a fortnight without a sighting, I started to suspect that either Mr Delaney's 'assets' had given him inaccurate information, or that if Frank Warner really had been spotted in The Bird In Hand, he must have left town since then.

*

The following evening, the Bird In Hand was as dead as a dodo; so exceptionally quiet, indeed, that the landlord decided to give Beth the night off. No sooner had we stepped out at around seven when I saw a man who was unmistakably Frank Warner heading straight for the pub, square on, as if Delaney's photo was making a beeline for me. He looked at me as he passed, for more than a few seconds, before stepping into the pub. I stopped in my tracks.

"What's the matter?"

"I've got to go back in."

"But I hardly ever get a free evening! I thought we could go to the cinema or something."

"I can't."

"Why not? If you want another beer we can go to some other place."

"It's not that, it's -"

"It's *what?*"

"Look, let me buy you a drink."

"In the pub I work in six days a week? Are you crazy?"

"I have to go back in and I'd rather do it with you. I can't explain now, but I will later, I promise."

"Jesus!"

She stamped her foot on the pavement before following me inside. Warner was at a corner table, nursing a pint of bitter, the pub's sole customer (which made me wonder where Delaney's assets had got to). I pointed to a table that was neither too close nor too far away.

"Let's sit here."

The landlord looked up.

"What's up Beth? Can't live without me?"

And he laughed. Beth turned on me, furious.

"You can sit where you bloody like! On your bloody own!"

Loud enough for both the landlord and Mr Warner to hear. Beth pushed the door open and quit the premises. Warner was looking at me:

"Have a drink, mate. It won't solve any problems, but it'll put them in their proper perspective."

A South London accent. Cargo pants, hiking boots and a black sweatshirt. Twenty he might have been, but he was built, as we used to say back then, like a brick shithouse. He was grinning. Unwittingly, Beth had given me the perfect helping hand.

"You've got a point there."

I ordered a Special Brew at the bar. Frank Warner pointed at it.

"You want to watch it with that stuff. It's got more sugar in it than a Christmas cake. Fast tracks the alcohol straight to your head."

Yer 'ead.

"It's a special occasion."

He laughed.

"Don't worry, she'll be back."

He gestured at his table.

"Sit here if you want to, mate. There's not exactly a lot of conversation being made in this place."

"Don't mind if I do," I said, hoping I was feigning nonchalance as I sat down in the wooden chair opposite Warner, who held out a hand. I shook it and said my name. He nodded.

"David," he said. So: the alias.

He asked me if I was a student and I said I was, but added that I was more interested in things other than my studies.

"Oh, and what might they be?"

"One of them just walked out on me and the other one is politics."

"Politics? What kind?"

When he heard I was with the RWP, he nodded, unsurprised.

"I joined that lot when I was sixteen and a half and got out when I was sixteen and three quarters."

"I know what you mean. But what else can one do?"

I bit my lip: that 'one' sounded too upper crust. He gave me a sly smile.

"Lots of things."

"For example?"

"Supergluing the entrances to the buildings of the powers that be. Bricking the windows of shops that treat their workers like shit. Etcetera. Nobody gets hurt, and points get made."

I now had the feeling – fool that I was – that we were getting on like a house on fire. If I hadn't thought that, I'd never have pushed the envelope.

"What about bombs?"

His eyes narrowed.

"I don't agree with bombs. Dangerous things, better left alone."

I blushed:

"Of course."

"Can I ask at which college you're studying?"

"Wolverton."

Again he nodded, in the same unsurprised fashion as when he'd heard I was in the RWP.

"And your subject is…?"

Small talk.

"English literature."

"Who's your tutor?"

He asked this in a way so imperative, I couldn't have answered any faster than if he'd been a policeman. Or a judge.

"Alan Curtis."

David nodded again, and snapped his fingers.

"Curtis."

He split the surname into two all but separate syllables. Curt. Is.

"I'd been told that might have been the case."

What?

"Really?"

He grinned again, and looked at his watch.

"Is there a phone in here?"

Knowing as I did every corner of the pub, I pointed him to the pay phone on the far side of the bar. The call took just over a minute, which I spent feeling nonplussed, given that the 'little chat' which Delaney had asked me to have with this man had turned into something rather odd that I couldn't quite put my finger on.

Frank – or David – came back to his seat. He was watching my eyes.

Then he leaned forward and stage-whispered:

"How about sharing a spliff outside?"

I wasn't much of a dope-smoker but there was something so peremptory about the way David had made the suggestion, it felt unadvisable to say no. So out through the swinging doors we went, into the stone smell of that university town. It was raining cats and dogs.

"We'll get soaked," I said, "We'd be better off in the pub."

No sooner had I started to turn than he clenched my arm.

"You're staying with me."

We waited, forcibly together, me now starting to panic, while a breeze flipped rain at us until, within minutes, we were drenched from head to toe. He stood ramrod straight, staring straight ahead, unfazed by the downpour. After not long, a four door Coca-Cola-coloured Hillman Avenger, shiny under the downpour, rounded the corner at full tilt and braked with a squeal. There was a woman at the wheel, her hair in a headscarf. David pulled my arm so hard, it hurt the socket. One of the back doors opened and I was half pushed, half-thrown onto the floor of the car, where two people immediately clamped their feet onto me, one pair on my legs, the other on my back. David snapped:

"Keep your face down!"

I heard the rear door slam, then the front nearside being opened and shut. Perplexed, with not a clue as to what was going on and much less as to what to do, I lay there. The car shot forward. My nose, squashed up against a latex carpet, started to hurt, so I turned it to the left. One of the four feet left my back and came down on my head.

"Not one move!"

A woman's voice.

"Put your safety belt on, David. Clunk fucking click or we'll all get nicked."

A man, in the back. A Northern Irish accent.

"Shit, forgot."

After a few minutes, an increase in speed and a hum of fast traffic indicated we were now on a motorway. By the time we got off it and the car drew up to heaven knew where, I calculated, despite my discomfort and confusion, that about an hour had passed. After a moment of silence, David said:

"Let's get him indoors. Janis, put your arm round him as you walk up to the house, all lovey-dovey. Warren, you stay on his left and me and Mavis'll walk ahead and unlock the door."

Mavis?

"And as for you…" I felt a finger poke my back, "keep quiet, look down at the ground and don't try anything funny."

The four doors swung open and the Irishman called Warren pulled me up into a sitting position.

"Don't keep Janis waiting."

Standing outside the car now was a woman of Indian or Pakistani or Bangladeshi origin.

Janis?

She reached in, gripped my wrists and tugged me up and out. David and the woman who'd driven – the one with the headscarf – had unclipped a low front gate and next thing I knew Janis and I were following them up a short path to the door of a terraced house. It was still raining. Janis had her arm around me, but there was nothing affectionate about her grasp or the way in which she propelled me up to the door and into a dark hall. Once inside, I was led into a living room whose curtains were drawn tighter than professor Curtis's, and pushed bumwards into an armchair, more confused and agitated than ever.

My four escorts sat down in turn, saying not a word, giving my eyes time to get used enough to the penumbra to locate

David on a sofa, with head-scarfed Mavis sitting next to him. The remaining man – the Irishman, Warren – and the remaining woman – South Asian Janis – were on separate chairs; Janis was frowning.

Warren said:

"That's one fucking big risk we've just run."

David said:

"Robert and Alice think it was worth it. And so do I."

Janis said:

"What if he doesn't want to help us?"

Mavis snapped:

"In that case, we'll make him."

David sighed:

"Mavis, *please*. We're not the Red Brigades."

"We're not the fucking CND, either!"

Warren rolled his eyes:

"Persuasion, Mavis, persuasion's the only way. It's not as if we don't have a cause."

By this time, I could see them all clearly. Head-scarfed Mavis, Irish Warren and South Asian Janis were in their early twenties, and so a little older than ex-soldier David. They all wore loose jumpers over wide open collars, suede or denim jackets, flared trousers and shoes with modest platforms.

"Where the fuck are the others?" Warren checked his watch, "They should be back by now."

A pause, during which I had time to notice how bare the room was: just them, their chairs and a low table with a small TV set on it. No pictures, no cupboards. My forehead was wet with sweat and my heart had started to syncopate.

The front door opened and clunked shut. Warren said:

"About time."

A black couple, in dark clothes, stepped into my line of vision. The man pointed at me.

"So you got him?"

Coming in behind them, a white couple entered the room. The man said:

"Well, hello there!"

I found myself staring, flabbergasted, at Ralph Finns, his face made older by a neatly preened beard. Sarah was standing next to him, almost unrecognisable, what with her black hair dyed blonde, leather trousers, tie-dye T-shirt and a biker's jacket:

"I imagine you had a pretty rough ride."

I opened my mouth to answer, but not a word came out. I finally managed to say:

"Ralph? Sarah?"

They shrugged.

"Robert and Alice, for the time being."

To the others, Sarah aka 'Alice' turned to the others:

"Robert and I need to put our friend in the picture. On our own."

71

Mavis said:

"How much in the picture?"

Ralph said:

"Completely."

"Are you sure?"

"Completely."

Janis said:

"I suppose we'll have to leave you to it, then."

The others abandoned the room. Sarah closed the door behind them. Ralph placed his face close to mine.

"Are you OK?"

As mystified as I was worried, I managed to say:

"I think so."

"Alice and I really didn't want an abduction, but the more security-minded among us thought it necessary. I imagine there are a few questions you might want to ask."

I waved at the curtained window.

"Where am I, Ralph?"

"Robert, please. Herne Hill, London. There's all sorts here. White English, Black English, Asian English. Quite a few squatters. Nobody stands out, everybody fits in. As for our current premises, they belong to a housing association, rented under a false name."

I gulped, wondering what it was they wanted from me. Or to do to me.

"Is this The Vanguard?"

Sarah and Ralph looked at me in that way people do when they don't need to answer.

"Ralph, and Sarah, you're in *The Vanguard?*"

It came out as a nervous whine. Ralph said:

"Please stick to the false monikers. It's safer. Like I said, I'm Robert and she's Alice."

Sarah spoke quietly:

"To answer your question, we are indeed in The Vanguard."

Ralph aka Robert smiled gently:

"As a matter of fact, we started it."

They waited for this to sink in, by which time I was ready to ask the question I wasn't sure I wanted to know the answer to.

"Why did you have me, well, kidnapped?"

Ralph frowned.

"Kidnap's too strong a word. Best case scenario, you have to stay until we've done what we're currently planning on doing, and then you're out of here, no questions asked."

Sarah smiled.

"But if our plan doesn't work…"

Ralph cut in:

"…which it might well not."

Sarah glanced irritably at Ralph:

"As I was saying, if it doesn't work – though I for one think it *will* – we would need to go to plan B. And if you wished, you could most definitely give us a helping hand with that."

Ralph's turn to smile.

"Let's say you're on stand-by."

Jesus Christ Almighty.

"But I don't know anything about explosives. And Ralph, I mean Robert here can confirm that I'm a lousy shot."

Both of them giggled, a little. Sarah's voice still had a chuckle in it when she said:

"No one's expecting you to turn into an urban guerrilla!"

My mind was thrashing around.

"So I'm here because of my Communist sympathies? Is that it?"

A flicker of condescension crossed Ralph's face.

"We're not Communists."

Then I remembered the well-thumbed books I'd seen at Clouds Manor: Kropotkin, Proudhon, Godwin, Stirner, Bookchin…

"Anarchists?"

"Nope."

Debord and Vaneigem and Jorn…

"Situationists, then?"

Sarah smiled:

"No -isms for us, though I won't deny that certain authors have given us some useful practical tips."

"But you call yourselves The Vanguard," I said, remembering something from an RWP meeting, "and that's a Leninist concept."

"Our little in-joke," she said, "it helps throw the police off the track. They've been asking all their informers in the Marxist parties to keep their ears well pricked up. In vain."

"Well," I said, flustered, "whatever you are, you can't deny you're violent. I mean, Ralph – Robert! – Sarah, I mean Alice, I'd never have thought you two, of all people would do that kind of stuff. I mean, Jesus, all those bombings, shooting at people's doors. And those churches. What was the point of *that?*"

Ralph said:

"We wanted to test an explosive more powerful than the ones we've been using up until now. A product that hails from Czechoslovakia. After much mulling, we came to the conclusion that churches would be easy, safe targets and would give us a fair idea of its relative effectiveness when compared to TNT. It turned out to be about one and a half times more powerful. I confess we overdid it in Wellingford; it was minor damage we were going for…"

How strange it was, to be talking thus with him, the erstwhile Burgundy drinker and Bang & Olafsen owner. I wondered what his exact role was. Choosing the targets? Planning the logistics? Planting the bombs, pulling the trigger?

"...after all, we didn't want to make mistakes like the Angry Brigade did with the Post Office Tower, did we? They went way over the top there. Could've killed someone."

Which he said in an offhand, common-sense way.

"So... you intend to go on planting bombs?"

Ralph paused, mouth open and still for a second or so before he said:

"Let's just say we're thinking ahead."

"And you blew up those churches just as an *experiment?*"

"Not a random one," said Sarah, "both churches were selected because of the confirmed misbehaviour of some members of their staff."

I was more bewildered than ever.

"What does that mean?"

Sarah said:

"We'll get round to that later on."

"What if you get caught? You could be jailed for the rest of your lives!"

"We know what we're doing."

Said without the smallest smidgen of doubt. I suddenly remembered him outdoors at Clouds Manor, downing magpies with precision. It struck me that for all I knew, he and Sarah might have been training with firearms for years. Then I remembered something else.

"Wait a moment. Aren't you two supposed to be in a tropical paradise?"

Ralph shook his head.

"But you got married somewhere exotic, with palm trees! It was in the papers!"

"Ever been to the Isles of Scilly? The Gulf Stream runs right by them. Palm trees galore. We never left the country. And we never got married, neither there nor anywhere else. Our press release was not altogether honest."

I went back to where they'd last left me.

"You said something about giving you a hand."

Ralph nodded:

"There's someone you know who could be essential."

I was more at a loss than ever.

"Me? *Who?*"

"Your tutor."

I almost stood up in surprise. I almost squeaked.

"*Professor Curtis?* What could he possibly have to do with anything?"

Sarah said:

"Let's put your tutor in context."

Ralph snorted:

"That's one way of expressing it."

His voice had become a touch shaky. Sarah didn't take her eyes off me.

"Ever heard of Unicorn Court?"

"Of course. It's that luxury estate in central London which you lot bombed a few weeks ago."

Sarah went on:

"What about Durham House and Owlcroft School For Girls, both in Preston?"

"I'd never heard of them until you bombed them as well."

"Quite so. OK, let's try some names. Raymond Gibson?"

"Doesn't ring any bells. What is all this about?"

"You'll see. What about Hugh Lowell?"

I stared at her.

"Is this some kind of joke?"

"No," Sarah said, "it's no joke. Do you know where his constituency is?"

"Somewhere up north. Liverpool?"

"Preston. What about Jimbo Johnson? Sebastian Hayley?"

"I do live on Planet Earth, you know."

"And of course you know Alan Curtis."

That didn't help.

"But what's he got to do with the other people you've mentioned, Hayley and Lowell and Johnson and the one I didn't know…?"

"Raymond Gibson," Sarah said, lips pursed. Ralph said:

"Most of their victims, for various reasons, can't speak up."

His voice, shakier.

Sarah:

"So we're going to do it for them."

I frowned at Ralph.

"Victims? What victims?"

Ralph sighed, took out a pack of cigarettes and offered one to Sarah (a slight tremor in his hand) then one to me (ditto).

"Smoke?"

"I don't."

He pocketed the pack, and she and he lit up. Ralph blew twin streams of Virginia out of his nostrils.

"Professor Curtis is an active member of a paedophile ring," Sarah said. Before my jaw could drop, Ralph added:

"And getting the boys isn't like falling off a log. We're not talking about prostitutes."

"We're talking about boys and girls aged mainly between eight and ten, sometimes eleven or twelve, tops."

"Who have to be brought to a convenient venue. It's not as if it's legal. It's not as if these children want to do this."

"So they look for vulnerable ones, often to be found in institutions like boys' hostels or approved schools for girls."

They weren't giving me a second for me to voice the astonishment which was now making such a huge racket in my head. *My tutor?*

"To do this, you need a procurer. Your professor uses a man called Raymond Gibson. A nod from Curtis, and Gibson will provide whatever is required by the fellow members of Curtis's circle: a single boy for a 'meeting' with a certain politician in a safe backroom; a couple of little girls to slide into the back of a TV entertainer's Rolls; a bevy of young lads for a full-blown shindig. You name it. Curtis, together with Gibson and the other people we've mentioned, has got quite a circus going."

Hugh Lowell, the cheery, down-to-earth MP. Jumping Jimbo, presenter of the homonymous popular show for children. Sarah said:

"With access to boys and girls who can then be moved to B&Bs, private homes or kept conveniently on the institutional premises where they live. And duly abused. Naturally, there are logistics that have to be dealt with. Transport, lodgings, food and drink – drink especially – for both for the clients and their victims. Gibson's good at that. A very efficient man. By the way, he used to go to the same prestigious university where Alan Curtis still teaches."

"He's got connections all over the place."

My mouth fuffed about:

"But…"

"But what?"

"I've never heard of this Gibson man. But Jimbo Johnson is watched every week by millions of kids and as often as not by their parents too! I grew up with him, for heaven's sake! I mean, if he'd been caught doing what you say he does with little boys, he'd have been put away years ago."

"What makes you think he only goes for boys?"

After a momentary loss for words, I said:

"What about Sebastian Hayley? I doubt the BBC would have let him have such a long run as a TV chef if he was a paedophile."

"You'd be amazed."

They didn't appear to be exaggerating.

"All right, just for the sake of argument, let's say that it's possible that Johnson and Hayley, extravagant show business types, I grant you, might have been involved in this ring of yours. But if I find it hard to accept that these incredibly popular figures have been abusing children, I simply cannot believe that a well-known, well-loved MP like Hugh Lowell could be a paedophile. And if I find *that* impossible, I mean imagine how I feel about professor Curtis, who's been my tutor for over a year, who's always been absolutely courteous and correct with me and his other students. In fact, I like him very much. And by the way, he's never made anything remotely resembling so much as a pass at me."

I rested my case, in this curtained off room, this chilly South London chamber to which I'd been forcibly removed with the compliance of someone I'd always thought of as a more-or-less friend.

Sarah smiled in a nurse-like way.

"You're too old."

"I just can't believe he…"

Sarah leaned forward.

"Believe it."

In a small voice, I asked:

"How long did you say this has been going on for?"

Sarah gave me another nurse-like smile:

"Donkey's years."

"And those churches?"

Ralph said:

"Their priests had their own self-sufficient little set-ups with some of the younger and more susceptible male members of their respective congregations; plus a few altar boys… We just thought we'd give said clergymen a bit of a kick up their arses."

Sarah added:

"They were a side-dish, if you like."

"It's the others we're really after."

A doubt flashed through what was left of my surprised mind.

"Meaning?"

"We want to expose them. What else?"

What else, indeed?

"I still really can't understand why they weren't all arrested a long time ago."

Ralph's turn to lean forward.

"Look at it from the point of view of the victims. *Think* about it: you're an eight-year-old living in a publicly-funded home where the food's disgusting and bullying is par for the course. One night, without warning, you are ordered out of bed at night by one of the wardens and taken forcibly to an isolated place – the basement of the same building, let's say – where a national treasure is waiting for you. He tells you to fellate him, in words he knows you'll understand. As you're scared out of your wits; and as the national treasure has already got it out and is shoving it into your mouth and giving you further instructions, you do as you're told. Afterwards, when you're back in your dormitory and staring at the ceiling, you feel worse than shit. Compared to you, in fact, shit looks pretty attractive. So it's your stinking, infantile word against that of a prestigious, universally loved man who nobody, not a single soul, is going to believe he could force a miserable little bastard like yourself to suck his dick."

His voice was laced with an unusual vehemence. As for me, the scene he'd just described was starting to paint an unprecedented, vivid picture in my head.

"But, if this has been happening for so long, at least some of the victims must now be adults. So are you telling me that *not one* of them has gone to the police?"

"Some. Not many."

"So what happened when they did?"

Ralph answered in a voice that was making an effort to be patient.

"*Nothing*. It's not considered, by those high up enough to do the considering, to be in the public interest to have a major politician or a beloved TV personality exposed as a kiddy fiddler. In the case of high-profile politicians, it's bad for the whole nation. And *very* bad for the entertainment business in the case of TV celebrities. So the accusations get passed on to a higher authority, which puts them in a safe and forgets the combination. Nobody wants to admit they've been involved at some level in a cover-up, so everybody's complicit, everybody keeps mum. Take your tutor, for instance. *Professor* Curtis. He was accused by one of his former victims, but his prestigious university and the local police ended up by giving each other a gentleman's handshake and dropping the matter: no one wanted that university to lose any of its considerable prestige."

"All right," I said, not feeling that any of this was in the least bit all right, "but Ralph, *Robert*, we're the same age and we went to the same school, and this is the first inkling I've had of any of this, yet you seem to know everything about it. And Sarah, *Alice*, I'm sorry, but the last time I saw you, you were working as a butleress at Clouds Manor and yet you're involved in this whole thing as well. I just don't get it. I just *don't*."

My face must have looked as if it really didn't, because they were wearing sympathetic expressions. Ralph said:

"We know people who know the abused."

"And we know," Sarah added, "some of the victims themselves."

Ralph smiled.

"And so do you."

Before you could ask who, the ex-soldier came to mind.

"David?"

"Well guessed. Who else, do you think?"

I shrugged.

"Mavis? Or Janis?"

Sarah grimaced.

"Both."

"Warren, maybe?"

"Warren is right," said Ralph, "One to go."

Who else was there?

"The black couple whose names I don't know, don't seem to be –"

"They're not. They're just, well, on our side."

"Still one to go," said Ralph.

"But that only leaves…"

I looked at Sarah, who shook her head.

"Ralph? *Ralph?*"

The vehemence I'd noticed earlier had fallen from his face.

"I was seven when my housemaster summoned me into his study for the first time, which I thought was odd, because I hadn't broken any rules and my schoolwork had been better than OK. He came out from behind his desk and said *I hear you've been misbehaving* and I said *in what way, sir?* and then he muttered *it doesn't matter in what way* and pushed me face down over his desk and I supposed I was going to get a caning, what else could I suppose?, but the next thing I knew he was yanking down my shorts and underpants and he smeared something on my arse and before I could even try to guess what it was I felt something hard jammed into me, I was so upset by the pain it took me a while to realise what the something hard was; he fucked me and fucked me until finally he grunted and pulled out; I didn't move, petrified and in pain, until he said *pull your pants up, you can't go out of here bollock naked can you?* So I turned around in time to see his fly being closed and I pulled up my pants and this man – thirty-something he was, back then – dug into his pocket, pulled out a packet of jelly babies and gave me one; *now, off you go.* He summoned me back to his study the following week. And," Ralph paused, made a gesture with one hand as if brushing off the memory, or trying to, "raped me again."

I shook my head, barely able to take this in.

"My God, how… many times?"

Another brush-off:

"After the fourth assault I finally went to the headmaster and told him what was happening and the headmaster got angry and told me not to tell fibs. So that same day, a Friday, it was always a Friday, I went back home and told my Dad that I wasn't going back under any circumstances, and why. He didn't, or couldn't, believe me. I had a bad weekend," Ralph shrugged, as if trying to make light of it all, "and when Monday rolled around, I was in a state. Looking back on it, I must have had some kind of nervous breakdown: I was crying, refused to get out of bed, lashed out when anyone tried to make me. Dad finally saw that there was more to this than had previously met his eye. He said that I could stay at home and that he'd look into it. A few days later he came into my room and told me that he'd hired someone – a private investigator, I assume – who confirmed that my housemaster was abusing not only me but also several other boys. Dad apologised to me, profusely, for not having believed me in the first place; for having sent me to that school in the first place."

Then and only then did I realise that, unusually for him, Ralph had been explaining all this without making any eye contact with either Sarah or me.

"Then he told me he had contacted the police but was told that the evidence, including that gathered by whoever it was he'd hired, was hearsay only," Ralph attempted a smile, his lips a tad a-tremble, "so it was just the school's word against that of the pupils, and the school, surprise, surprise, denied everything. And my housemaster, surprise, surprise, had already moved or been moved on to some other place which everybody claimed not to know. So the police shelved any investigation they might or might not have been thinking of making. The next day Dad turned up with a pile of prospectuses, and I eventually opted for the school where you and I met. Dad felt so guilty about the whole thing, that he started to spoil me something rotten. He still does. It turned out that Sarah, who had believed me when I first told her, had – for reasons of her own, which she is not at liberty to disclose – already been getting in touch with several other victims of other abusers in other places and at other times, who wanted to lift the lid on their tormentors for good, no matter how powerful they were, no matter who was covering up for them. To do something that would make other abusers think twice."

Ralph bowed his head, and sighed. Sarah said:

"And we're going to do it."

His face puckered up into a steadfast frown, Ralph muttered:

"So we are."

His head was now shaking slightly from side to side. I was still wondering about Sarah: what could those reasons of hers be? She broke in:

"No prizes for guessing the name of Robert's abuser."

I nodded.

"None required."

I could see him as clearly as if he were sitting in the same room, in his dark brown suit and black lace-up Oxfords of the type my grandfather used to wear. Ralph said:

"He's the person you can help us with."

Sarah added:

"Should that be necessary."

*

Then he and Sarah sat back on their simple wooden chairs and watched me on mine; there in the penumbra. I found myself staring at the floor, amazed that I had never suspected that something like this could have happened to Ralph. After all, I thought I knew him fairly well. Yet I'd never spotted any chink in his armour, never so much as had one iota of suspicion that something so unthinkably bad might have been done to him.

I'd read about child abuse in my parents' Sunday supplements and I knew that in the UK it was more widespread than previously believed. But it had never occurred to me that it took place beyond dark little local levels; that the rich and famous and prestigious and scholarly might be at it too: that the highest echelons of English society might be indulging their sexual appetites with unwilling children and then making sure everybody involved kept quiet about it.

It was only then that, for the first time in my life, I started to think hard about the victims. To really imagine what they had been through. The little boys, the little girls, children the rest of whose lives were not going to be in the least bit joyous, having been forced to start them the way they had. In some cases by men whose innocence I had taken for granted; whose programmes I had watched with the thoughtless admiration I had always felt for them; or with the particular respect I felt for Hugh Lowell MP whenever he made an appearance, because of the way he always spoke straight from the hip, in a way most MPs never did, with an accent most MPs never had; and now, the mental gloss I had always used in order to emulsion the smiling chef, the prancing children's entertainer, the cheery right honourable gentleman from the north, had dried, cracked, snapped, splintered and fallen, in smithereens, to the floor, which I now looked up from because Ralph was muttering something all but inaudible which, once I'd pricked up my ears, turned out to be:

"It hurt so much. Here."

He floppily patted the crown of his head, and all I could see now was professor Curtis, sitting before me, his smile so understanding as I fumbled through an essay on Wordsworth or Coleridge. He who had done *that* to the friend in front of me. Sarah said:

"Let's give you a minute or two. I think you need it."

She wasn't wrong: I sat in that darkened space, feeling by turns naïve, disappointed, disgusted and shocked, until Ralph and Sarah's words ended up sinking into me bodily, or so it felt, until all the wishy-washiness that until then had been the stock in trade of my state of mind drained out of me with a definitive gurgle.

A mind which a moral imperative had already made up, before I had even taken account of the risks involved. Followed by an immediate account-taking of the risks. Followed by the certainty that if I didn't take them, I would nor could ever forgive myself.

"If I can be of any help at all, you only have to let me know. But first, though, there's something I need to tell you."

*

Half an hour later, Ralph and Sarah called the others back. They sat down and watched me with stony faces, slowly blinking eyes, legs crossed or stretched out in front of them; it struck me now how little I really knew any of them: where they came from, what they had done; or had had done to them.

Ralph said:

"We've explained everything. He wants to help. I can vouch for him one hundred per cent."

I blushed. Mavis, the woman with the headscarf, snapped:

"You sure?"

Ralph snapped back:

"Yes. And that is *that*."

Silence. Sarah turned to me:

"You said that there was something you had to tell us?"

I explained that one James Delaney, an MI5 mole in the Real Workers' Party, had 'recruited' me and asked me to try and engage David in conversation. A wave of muttering and exclamations swept across the room. David gave a laugh which wasn't a laugh at all.

"Are you saying that you were looking for me at the same time as I was looking for you?"

Complicated. They were looking at me with a seriousness I had instinctively begun to mirror.

"Well… apparently. How did you recognise me?"

"Robert here gave me a description that was sufficiently detailed. How did *you* recognise *me?*"

"Delaney gave me a photograph."

David leaned forward.

"They have a *picture* of me?"

"From when you were in the army."

"Did this man say exactly why he was interested in me?"

"He said you'd been an explosives expert in the SAS and that you'd gone – what's it called when soldiers go missing?"

"AWOL."

"That. Which made them suspicious, because they assumed The Vanguard must have at least one person with your kind of expertise."

"Were they *sure* I was involved?"

"No. An educated guess, he said."

Mavis cut in:

"And why did this man choose *you* to talk to David?"

"I'm in the Real Workers' Party. And as you…"

I pointed to David.

"…were in it too, Delaney thought that would give me a talking point. That's all he wanted, for me to talk with you. About anything, but preferably politics. Or that's what he said."

All heads turned David's way. Northern Irish Warren said:

"You were in the *RWP*, David?"

Janis and Mavis giggled. David coughed, his face reddening.

"Not for very long, I wasn't."

Warren said:

"There's nothing to laugh about. This man Delaney suspects David and is probably looking for this temporary recruit of his, as we speak."

A nod at me.

Mavis said:

"We need to take out the spook."

David muttered:

"Take out, take out... we're not the Baader-Meinhof gang."

"Last time it was the Red Brigades."

"Whatever. We simply need to *neutralise* this handler in some way..."

He paused, thinking.

"...or let the authorities do it themselves."

"The authorities?"

"It's a possibility."

"This another one of your crazy schemes, David?"

"It's not so crazy."

He turned to me:

"Do you know where we might find Mr Delaney?"

In the crosshairs of their serious looks, I felt I needed to do something more to prove myself, to help assuage the suspicions which I sensed that some of them still held, even though I'd been vouched for, even though I'd already given them some possibly useful information. I spoke almost comically fast:

"Yes! In his guise as an RWP official, he gives a talk in Wellingford every Thursday at 6pm at the Matthew Arnold auditorium. For two more weeks."

David turned to the black woman.

"Do you think you could get to Mr Delaney's next talk, and inveigle him into a friendly chat after the event?"

She frowned.

"*How* friendly?"

Nobody laughed. David said:

"Maybe suggest you'd like to buy him a drink. Maybe suggest, while drinking, that you'd like to see him again. Maybe even, I don't know, at his place."

She balked.

"I'm not going to shag him."

"No one's suggesting that you do, Stevie. What we need is to get some idea of how much he knows. And, if at all possible, to find some way of keeping him out of our hair."

"That's a tall order if ever there was one."

"Just whatever you can manage. No more, no less."

She gave a what-else-can-I-do shrug.

"If you insist."

David stood up.

"I reckon we're done for now. Everybody knows what the next step is. After which we'll need a day or two, to wait for the results."

The black man said:

"And if we don't get any, how long have we got for the next stage?"

"A month, at most."

A collective gasp. Warren said:

"*Four weeks?* That's impossible."

Sarah wagged a dismissive finger.

"No it's not, now that we've got this man to help us out."

She placed a hand on my shoulder. As I wondered what she meant by that, Ralph said:

"Talking of which, now he's with us he's going to have to take on a name," he turned to me, "All very cloak and dagger, I know, but our aliases need to become so automatic that we don't drop them for a moment on the outside."

I found this a touch absurd, but Ralph sounded so convinced that it reduced the risk of being caught, I was happy to give him the benefit of the doubt.

"Can I ask how you choose yours? At random?"

"Not exactly."

Ralph or 'Robert' pointed at himself, and said:

"Plant."

Sarah or 'Alice' did the same.

"Cooper."

Irish Warren said:

"Zevon."

Headscarfed Mavis:

"Staples."

Ex-soldier David:

"Bowie."

South Asian Janis:

"Joplin."

The black couple waved from their sofa:

"Stevie and Van. You can guess the rest."

Ralph nodded at me.

"So, who do *you* like?"

I settled for Lou.

PART TWO: READY

VIII

On an autumn day in 1977, London's sky is the colour of an unwashed sheet and most people are walking around in anoraks or crombies or donkey jackets. A man in a sheepskin coat approaches the grey stone entrance arch of Thames House on Millbank. He goes through a metal detector and takes a lift to the third floor, where he enters an office lined with dark wood and says good morning to a besuited, late-middle-aged man with portly cheeks and eyes the colour of cockles.

"Well, if it isn't agent Red Flag, in the flesh," the man says in impeccable public schoolese. "Do sit down."

Delaney does so in one of the two padded mahogany chairs facing the man's desk.

"Thank-you, Sir Michael." His accent is equally impeccable, bereft of any Liverpudlian traces. Sir Michael leans back and taps a cardboard file on his desk.

"According to reports recently received, I am given to understand that a temporary recruit of yours has, as it were, been mislaid."

"Well, I wouldn't say that, exactly" says Delaney.

"Well, what *would* you say? And where were your so-called assets when this happened?"

His unruffled demeanour notwithstanding, Sir Michael's tone reveals that he is in what at Delaney's old Alma Mater would have been called a bate.

"Unfortunately, one man wasn't on duty that night and the other was down with the 'flu."

"Are you telling me your temporary recruit was left *on his own?*"

"I later spoke on the phone to the landlord of the public house in which the recruit had succeeded in engaging the target in conversation. He informed me that both the recruit and the target left the premises soon afterwards."

"And?"

"I suspect that the target then took the recruit away from the immediate area, possibly through the use of force."

"Are you telling me the recruit's been kidnapped?"

"Let's say that that can't be ruled out."

Sir Michael slaps his file.

"Let's say that this is one god-awful mess. Does the recruit have a girlfriend, wife, partner, boyfriend?"

"He's been seeing the barmaid who works at the same pub. But she wasn't there when he and the target left."

"Isn't she concerned? Mightn't she start looking for him? Or report his disappearance to the police?"

"I approached her the following day, in my role as a member of the RWP. I told her the recruit had decided to go with his caucus on a two-week seminar in London on Historical Materialism and hadn't had time to tell her."

"Sounds pretty spurious to me; still, I suppose a barmaid might swallow it. What about his family?"

"He only calls his parents once every two or three weeks, so for the time being, at least, they won't be suspecting anything's amiss."

Sir Michael stares at Delaney.

"That target was the only plausible lead we had for the Vanguard. And your recruit's disappearance suggests to me that we were right. What a pity that you don't have a clue as to their whereabouts."

"I'm sorry, Sir Michael, I –"

"Let's just hope nothing untoward happens to the recruit. Christ only knows the fuss the Press would kick up if this boy were to be found dead in a ditch."

"I –"

"Shut up."

Sir Michael picks up the phone.

"Peter? Michael here. Listen, the man we put on the Vanguard case has made a right regal cock-up…" Sir Michael turns his cockle-coloured eyes on Delaney, "Listen, why don't I run you through the details later at that new club you're always talking about…? Six would be fine."

He puts down the phone.

"As you got us into this situation, we don't see why you shouldn't try to get us out of it. So get back to work. And find some assets who aren't liabilities."

"Sir –"

"Shut up. The door's over there."

IX

I was still half asleep in the bedroom they'd assigned me, twitching from a draught, when I heard voices in the corridor and the sound of people trooping downstairs. So I put on my shoes and followed them into the living room. Ralph and Sarah were the last to enter, plucking out sheets of A4 paper from plastic folders. Sarah looked at me:

"Lou, we're going to go over certain things that don't involve you. I'm sorry…"

She raises her hands apologetically.

"…but I'm going to have to ask you to leave."

"No problem, I know when I'm not wanted."

An attempt to be flippant. I squeezed my way past the others, back into the corridor. Not wanting to be suspected of eavesdropping, I went over to the kitchen, which whiffed of recently fried egg. An open tub of margarine and a packet of sliced bread were on the kitchen table, and not having had breakfast, I took a yellow-smeared knife and served myself a slice. Not long after that, I felt what my grandmother used to call a call of nature. I headed upstairs to the toilet, unsure as to why, instinctively, I found myself trying not to make the steps squeak. Up on the first floor, I pulled open the nearly identical door next to the one for the toilet and found myself looking into a broom cupboard in which there weren't any brooms at all but several assault rifles placed on vertical racks. After a few seconds I recognised the Finnish gun Ralph had let me use at Cloud Manor and the one with which I'd seen Ralph take out a couple of bottles and a brace of magpies.

Stacked on the cupboard floor were piles of plastic-wrapped orange slabs, labelled SEMTEX-H. On top of each pile were some wires connected to thin, pen-like sticks. Four or five alarm clocks had been dumped in a corner, higgledy-piggledy; a dozen or so two-inch metal pipes were lying neatly in the opposite corner. Nature had ceased to call.

"Lou!"

I hurried back downstairs, where Ralph was waiting for me.

"Come on in!"

I went back into the living room. Sarah was saying:

"…it would be safer for the plan if we went outdoors in disguise, but without looking as we've just walked out of a joke shop. Janis?"

"I didn't spend two years as a make-up girl at Thames Television for nothing. But I'll need a proper kit. We're talking a hundred, hundred and fifty quid."

David turned to Ralph.

"I think the bank can meet that."

"It can."

Sarah went on:

"Stevie, are you set?"

Up she stood.

"On my way."

X

James Delaney hurries past grey-stone college buildings (many years ago, it was on one of these streets that Delaney himself had been recruited by a middle-aged, kindly-sounding man who went by the name of Maurice) stops in front of the pub his recruit used to frequent, and takes a good look around. The other houses on the square are large Victorian residences, now divided into flats. Delaney takes a wallet out of his back pocket and plucks out an ID card that will be, he considers, just the ticket.

*

After posing as a CID Detective Inspector for three hours, and having doorstepped – he calculates – about four dozen potential witnesses, he has one bona fide piece of data. A dark-coloured late model Hillman Avenger – woman driver, two passengers – was speeding in the vicinity, then stopped to pick up a couple of men who were waiting in front of The Bird In Hand. The witnesses were too far away to make out the number plate. One said the driver was wearing a 'hippy-type headscarf'.

In other words, sweet FA. Still, thinks James Delaney, I'll put the word out. I'll clutch at this straw.

He locates an empty phone box reeking of chilled urine, and calls Millbank.

*

"I don't want to speak to the secretary, I want to speak to Sir Michael in person. Identify myself? I've already told you my code name is Red Flag… What? The password? I've gone blank." He slaps his forehead. "Couldn't you give me a clue of some kind? It's vital that I get through to him. I'm an undercover officer, for God's sake! The name of a friendly fish? A guppy? A goldfish? What? It begins with a P…? I've got it! Porpoise! Porpoise! And it's not a fish, by the way, not strictly speaking. Now can I speak to Sir Michael?" The hand holding the receiver is sweating, even though the rest of him isn't. "Sir Michael, good to hear your voice, sir. About the affair in hand, I've been doing a little digging. Both the target and the recruit were picked up by a late model dark-coloured Hillman Avenger. The driver was a woman, and was wearing a hippyish headscarf. Mm? That would be like a kind of bandanna, sir. What colour? The scarf or the woman? The witnesses didn't say, so she must have been white. I know it's not much, sir. No number plate, no. Yes, I know it's not enough and I will definitely keep on digging. Thank-you and good –"

Sir Michael hangs up in mid-farewell. His tone has been dismissive going on downright rude. James Delaney steps out of the phone box. He doesn't have a clue as to where to look next. His spirits sink, suddenly. *Christ*, he thinks, *I need a drink.*

XI

Beth dips glasses into the rotating washer, thinking that there was something fishy about that skinny man from the Real Workers' Party who came in yesterday to talk about her new-found boyfriend. To start with, this stranger's Liverpudlian accent was definitely off, false, affected; on top of which, Beth knows that her boyfriend is not the kind of person who'd take himself off to a seminar in London without saying a word to her (and even less, leave it to that fake scouser to tell her where he's gone). She dunks the last unclean glass and wipes the bar. 12.30, and not a customer in sight.

She dumps the cloth, goes to the pub's phone and calls up the Real Workers' Party's central office. It takes her but ten minutes to confirm that the RWP isn't holding any seminar on Historical Materialism – or anything else – anywhere whatsoever in the Greater London area.

So: something has happened to her boyfriend that she doesn't know about. Something odd. Which begs the question: what can she do about it?

In less than a minute, she finds the answer.

XII

Every one of the Matthew Arnold auditorium's fifty seats is taken and the standing room is packed rush-hour tight. A shadow moves onto the stage and a sudden spotlight reveals Delaney in his usual black gear, although anyone paying close attention would notice that his shirt is unbuttoned at the midriff, and that the jacket has a few ash stains, and that his shoes are scuffed. He begins with a smile that comes across as sheepish as he starts his talk:

"Today's subject, as I announced last week, is the police. What can we say about them?"

He shakes his head.

"Let's begin at the beginning. There used to be no police, just a few conchtables, constables, and a few night washmen. In London, for example, in the eighteenth shentury, century, there were about a hundred night washmen for every conchtable and they were paid exclusively by the local authorities. There were no professional police paid for by the state until Sir Robert Peel introduced the I can't remember the exact name of what Act in eighteen twenty-two. I think. Or maybe it was eighteen thirty-two. I jush can't remember. Mush be getting old, ha ha ha!"

Whispers creep into the auditorium's silence.

"Anyway, who gives a flying fuck about the dates?"

His pronunciation comes out posh: 'fack'. His audience titters uncertainly.

"What matters is that not in the hishtory of mankind has a body of uniformed people been so utterly, *utterly* uselesh. The police, ladies and gennelmen, couldn't organise a pish-up in a brewery, an orgy in a brothel, or a bun fight in a bleeding bakery. And every last mother's bashtard of them has the IQ of a brillo pad. I wouldn't trust a policeman – or a policewoman, for that matter – to work as a facking lollipop lady. So fack 'em all, that's what I say! Fack 'em side –"

He stops, because a hand has been placed on his arm, belonging to a person he suddenly recognises as the top RWP official at the university and the organiser of the event, whose other hand is now slapped over the mike.

"James, look, I don't know what's gotten into you today – or rather I know exactly what's gotten into you – but it'd be better if you stopped here. I've already thought of an excuse."

"But I've never felt better in my wife!"

"You have to leave the stage, James. Now."

"Shit. If you inshist."

The official nods and takes his hand off the mike into which Delaney immediately screams:

"The police are a bunch of facking wankers!"

112

More doubtful titters. He leaves the stage, leaving the official to proffer his pre-prepared story about the speaker being indisposed. The last word gets a laugh.

*

Delaney exits the venue ashamed of himself, aware (for the first time) that he has been drinking so much so that he completely forgot about his talk until the last minute and went onstage when he was in no condition to even be in the audience. He takes stock. The RWP official, he knows, will report his behaviour to the Central Committee, which might well expel him from the party, which would mean months of carefully planned infiltration up the flue, which in turn – the thoughts somersault through his still befuddled brain – might combine with the unexplained disappearance of his recent recruit to make Sir Michael doubt the wisdom of continuing to employ this particular officer.

"You're right."

He looks up. A truly attractive young black lady is smiling at him.

"About what?"

"The police *are* a bunch of fucking wankers."

The widening of her smile makes her more attractive still and her casual use of the word 'fucking' has him suddenly imagining doing just that with her.

"Oh. It wasn't a good talk, I'm afraid. I wasn't feeling very well."

The woman makes an I'm-pretending-to-think-about-it grimace.

"You looked a little short on self-confidence, but hey, you put your take on the pigs up there. I thought that was pretty brave, considering they probably had a plainclothes in the audience."

Brave?

"Thank-you."

"Listen, I was wondering if you'd care to go for a drink?"

Delaney tries to remember the last time a woman made a pass at him and comes up with a blank. A drink? Hell, one more won't hurt.

*

She takes him to a pub he's never been to before, with garish wall colours, too-loud music and a clientele younger than he is. He buys the drinks, not wanting her to pay for – or question – his choice of a triple Southern Comfort, and as he places her glass of rosé in front of her he takes in her smooth skin, her lively eyes, her irresistible smile. Once they've taken a couple of sips, she says:

"Man, you *really did* lay into the pigs."

The Southern Comfort instantly joins up with whatever he'd been tippling before his lecture (what was it?). Perplexing though he finds it that this gorgeous young woman doesn't think he's made an arse of himself onstage, the fact is she clearly doesn't. It occurs to him – his neurons do a quick jig – that he might be in with a chance here. A second jig provides him with a tall tale that might do the trick.

"Are you in the RWP?"

"Yes," she says, without batting an eyelid.

"Well," he says, "I have a little confession to make, but please don't tell the comrades!"

Playfully pursing her lips – so adorable! – she says:

"Mum's the word."

"My girlfriend's just ditched me. Which is why I went on stage a little too lubricated."

"And there was I," she says, "Thinking: poor guy, he's got a speech impediment."

Delaney laughs, loudly.

"Normally, I can hold my liquor pretty well. Talking of which, let me get another one of these," he raises his empty glass, "how about you?"

Her rosé is all but untouched.

"I'm fine."

He returns, taking a long sip before he sits down.

"Yeah," he says, "splitting up is kind of tough."

"Had you been together very long?"

A thoughtful pause.

"Couple of years."

"Oh. Poor you."

Complicit cow eyes.

"Well, time heals all wounds and all that."

"Sometimes it takes more than just time."

A silky tone, sparkling eyes. But before he can ask her what it is she has in mind, precisely, another female voice breaks in on the conversation:

"Why did you lie to me?"

Both of them look up at a wispy-haired blonde, standing at their table, furious. She is, Delaney knows, vaguely familiar. When she points a finger at him, the penny drops and his face starts to twitch uneasily.

"I followed you from your ridiculous lecture. Why did you tell me my friend was at an RWP seminar in London? There aren't any!"

This so loud, that even in the flurry of music and chatter inside that pub, people look around. The black lady takes a pen out of her jacket and scribbles a number on a beer mat, omitting to mention that it belongs to a phone box two blocks away.

"Beverly. Call me. Soon."

She smiles at Delaney before standing up and taking her leave. The blonde girl, who hasn't paid any attention to Beverley, shouts:

"Well? So where is he?"

Delaney rubs his eyes, behind which he can feel his brain bubbling and sloshing wearily, a stone's throw from throwing in the towel.

"I don't know, I really don't. I wish I did, I really do."

Beth sits down opposite.

"I want an answer: why did you lie?"

Delaney looks at her intense blue eyes boring into his and feels a desire as sudden as it is intense to be rid of her. So that he can call Beverley as soon as possible. He stands up, shakily, and says the first thing that comes into his head.

"The party has launched an independent investigation. We don't want any non-member interfering with it, to ensure…"

To ensure what?

"…that said investigation will not be interfered with. Look, I have to go."

He swigs down the remains of his drink and walks out. As the door closes behind him she shouts:

"Jammy bastard!"

*

No sooner does Delaney get back to his flat than he pulls Beverley's beer mat out of his pocket and gives her a call. He was thinking about her when on his way home. The way she just popped up out of nowhere. The way she flirted. The way she left him her number so casually. The fact that she's black. Must be a professional. Stands to reason. And he needs some fun, what with his investigation going nowhere and him having made a drunken fool of himself onstage.

"Beverley?"

"Speaking."

"It's James, from the RWP."

"Hello, James."

"I know this sounds a bit precipitate, but I was wondering if you'd like to come for dinner at my place?"

A pause.

"Sounds great, James."

"Eight-thirty?"

"What's the address?"

*

As she crosses the threshold, Stevie notes that Delaney's little flat – white radiators, armchairs, sofa, coffee table with nothing on it – is neat and tidy. Next to the coffee table, a foldable table for two has been set up, on which Delaney is placing napkins and a lit candle.

"Hi there, Bev. Let me hang up your jacket for you."

She removes her jacket, thinking: on abbreviated terms already, are we?

He hangs it on the hook at the entrance, then takes a bottle of Bulgarian red from the kitchen, opens it in front of her, fills the two glasses, and gestures to one of the table's two wooden chairs.

"Please…"

Delaney then fetches a large salad and places it on the table.

"I'm not exactly Sebastian Hayley, I'm afraid; I hope it'll be enough."

"I'm sure it will."

They get through the salad in silence.

"Thank-you, James, that was very nice."

He wipes his mouth with a paper napkin.

"You're welcome. Now, down to business."

"Business?"

"Come on, Bev," he says, "I wasn't born yesterday. I know a working girl when I see one, discreet though you are."

He slips his wallet out of his back pocket, and lays five tenners on the table.

"What do you say? Or should I add some more?"

Stevie's eyes have widened considerably.

"What makes you think I'm a hooker?"

Delaney smiles lopsidedly.

"The way you came on to me today, leaving your phone number, just like that, and, besides, most of the prostitutes around here are black; I suppose they're short of the readies, like so many black people, sadly. Here, let's top this up…"

He slaps two more tenners onto the pile.

"…that should be enough for anal and all. And don't worry, the rubbers are on me."

He stands up and points at a door.

"Bedroom's through there."

He comes round to her side of the table and tugs at her hand.

"Come on, I'm in need of a good fuck."

She rises to her feet.

"Are you now?"

"God, yes. The last few days have been hell."

"Just a minute, there ought to be some preliminaries, don't you think?"

She pulls him toward her.

"Preliminaries?"

"You know, foreplay."

Another lopsided smile.

"Of course."

120

"Well, then."

And she knees him full in the groin. As he buckles forward, yelling, she places her hands on his shoulders and pushes him back down onto his chair.

"I started doing self-defence classes when I was eleven," she says, "in the neighbourhood I was brought up in, you needed them."

She fishes something out of her pocket.

"You've made this easier for me than I could ever have imagined."

She gives the hardest slap she can to one side of his head, followed by another to the other. As his brain flops about in its cerebrospinal fluid, she pops three blue pills into his mouth then takes his most recent, still mainly full glass, pushes his head back and pours it down his throat.

"Triazolam. Mild sleeping pill. So mild, I'm giving you three."

He gurgles and tries to wave his arms.

"There, there, James."

She holds him down by the shoulders until, after a few minutes, the pills start to take effect. When his lids fall to half mast, she lets him go, fishes about in his pockets until she finds his keys, goes out and locks him in.

A couple of hundred yards on, she stops to make a phone call.

PART THREE: SUSPICION

XIII

Durham House in Preston is a light-grey pebble-dash affair, with half a dozen net-curtained windows on one side and three of the same at the front. There are scorch marks on one wall, left over from the bomb attack.

Van can't be standing there all day, it being brass monkey weather up here in Lancashire. He crosses over and finds the entrance – two black posts with a black gate swung open – and as he is about to cross the threshold he nods at a lone man loitering on the opposite side of the road, holding a small black case. David nods back.

Van steps through some swinging doors with wired glass windows set into them and heads for reception. It's a small office, with a glass window which the woman behind it now slides open.

"I'm looking for my nephew. Campbell, with a P. Christian name Winston."

She shakes her head.

"There are no coloured boys at Durham. And I'm not being racist."

"But his own mother told me he'd been sent here."

"Then his own mother was mistaken. Durham is a hostel for troubled but bright boys and we don't have any blacks."

"Are you saying that black boys can't be bright?"

Van's voice has risen. His face has taken on the caricatural demeanour of an angry Negro: bulging eyes, lips scrunched up, jaw stuck out. The woman immediately presses a button on her desk. A bell rings, muffled, in the depths of the building.

"Maybe the warden can help you," the woman says, alarm ruffling her face. The man checks his watch and gives the slightest of nods.

The warden turns out to be a youngish man in jeans and a jumper.

"Everything all right, Doris?"

"This gentleman is looking for a cousin of his, but I've already told him –"

"No bright black boys in *this* school," says Van, still putting on his face.

"That's right, I'm afraid, but it's not because we want it that way…"

The altercation goes on for a good twenty minutes, until Van checks his watch again and says:

"Perhaps I've made a mistake, after all. I'll double check with my sister."

Without a word more, he takes his leave. Back outside, he waits until David squeezes himself out of a basement window and dusts himself off.

"All right?"

David nods:

"Planted."

XIV

James Delaney hears the word faintly at first, as if called through thick glass; then louder but oddly indistinct, as if shouted through a letterbox.

"Clear!"

"Clear!"

"Clear!"

He thinks of the Scientologists, who do something, he vaguely remembers, called going clear. He licks the inside of his mouth, which is dry as stale bread, then hears a series of thumps followed by a sound like several bookshelves being pushed over at once. He opens his eyes.

His flat has been made tinier than it already is by the presence of half a dozen policemen in caps and pantomime-chubby bullet-proof vests, all of them pointing handguns at him, inches from his face.

"Stand up, with your hands where we can see them!"

He rises on shaky feet, his hands where they can see them. His arms are then forced down behind his back, his wrists feel cold metal and he hears a click. He is pushed back down into his chair. One of the policemen remains standing in front of him. The others are staring at a spot just behind him. Their sergeant whistles and points:

"Bloody hell, are those primed?"

What?

"What?"

A damaged whisper. The sergeant pulls him back onto his feet turns him round, and prods his chest bone so hard it makes him gulp.

"Are they fucking primed?"

Delaney now sees without believing that he's seeing half a dozen little orangey-yellow packs labelled 'Semtex-H', stacked neatly in one corner and topped by a pack of thin tubes with wires sticking out of them, held together by a rubber band.

"Are they fucking *primed?*"

Delaney looks at the explosives and the detonators, as bewildered as if they were a previously invisible litter of kittens.

"I don't think so."

"Get this bastard out of here. We're evacuating the building."

Two of the men holster their guns and drag Delaney over to the door.

XV

Jumping Jimbo Johnson walks out of his Cheyne Walk flat and plonks himself down in the driving seat of his new Jaguar SD1, undoing the buttons of the jacket of his trademark harlequin-themed suit so he can breathe more easily, his paunch becoming as it is more of a burden with every year that passes. He leans forward a moment and lets out a long, loud fart before turning the key in the ignition. His four concentric titanium necklaces tinkle a touch as he pulls away from the kerb and takes a route he knows like the back of his hand, the one that will lead, after just under a couple of hours, to his thatched country cottage on the outskirts of Aylesbury. A snatch of dialogue from a novel that professor Alan Curtis lent him comes to his mind. *"Yes, I have fucked a little girl." "Did you burst her in the very depths of her feeling?"*

"In her depths," he mutters, "and what's wrong with that, I'd like to know?"

He clicks on the radio and gets Paul Anka, with whom he starts to sing along:

"You're havin' my baby, what a lovely way of saying how much you love me, you're havin' my baby, what a lovely way to say that you're thinking of me…"

He raises his voice in synch with Anka's.

"*…'I can SEE IT, his face is GLOWING…'*"

He rolls onto the A413 and goes into fourth.

"'*…I can see it in your EYES that –*'"

"Keep yours on the road."

A man's voice. Johnson stiffens but doesn't take his eyes off the road: he's doing eighty. The whatever it is that's being pressed against the side of his neck is chilly as newly applied Vaseline.

"This is a Beretta twenty-two. Useless though it may be at more than twenty paces, it's effective at close range."

"And you're nice and close." A woman's voice. "Turn first right at the next roundabout, onto Hale Road. You know where that is, don't you?"

Johnson nods.

"'Course you do."

Johnson goes down to second and takes the turning.

"Now," says the woman, "keep going 'til you get to the turning for Hale *Lane*. You know where that is, don't you?"

Another nod.

"'Course you do."

Johnson swings onto the lane.

"Head for Wendover Woods," says the man.

"Nice and quiet at this time of day," says the woman. "As I know you know, Jimbo."

Johnson, sweating, now turns the car onto an asphalted path that quickly dwindles into a muddy track surrounded by trees.

"Stop the car."

Johnson switches the engine off and pulls up the handbrake. The woman says:

"Get out."

The woman and the man have already done so, watching as Johnson emerges, shoulders stooped, and clunks his door shut. Looking their way, he sees they are wearing balaclavas and surgical gloves. The man glances around.

"Still too public for me."

A Northern Irish accent.

IRA?

The woman nods at the trees.

"Into the woods, Jimbo."

Wiping back black hair brilliantined with perspiration, Johnson's two-tone shoes tread along the muddy path, into the woodland. The man and woman follow until the little group is surrounded by thick trunks. The man points his pistol at Johnson's head.

"On your knees."

"Oh God."

Mavis points at the Jaguar.

"Your car's parked right at the spot where the minibus from Owlcroft School in Preston dropped off us eight to ten-year-olds so we could get picked up by you and your friends, in their Rovers, Jags, Bentleys and Aston Martins. Right, Jimbo?"

A nod followed by a sniff.

"And then we'd be transferred to Unicorn Court in London. *Central* London. We'd be taken up to a ritzy flat, get plied with cigarettes and drink – not beer, mind, but the hard stuff: whisky, gin, vodka – and then we would be ushered into the estate's private indoor swimming pool, to which these people had a key. And once there…"

Mavis pauses for breath.

"…well it was anything goes, wasn't it, Jimbo? Skinny dipping. Feeling us up. Making us stick our fingers up your anuses while we fellated you. Straight sex. Even buggery. Buggery with little girls. How many of those outings were you involved in, Jimbo?"

The harlequined shoulders attempt a shrug.

"I don't know…"

"We ourselves – and we haven't forgotten a single one of those parties – have calculated twenty-four over a two-year period. And we know that there were dozens of others which we were lucky enough not to be at."

Mavis's voice has risen. She reaches a hand out to Warren.

"Give me the gun."

132

Warren keeps it aimed at Johnson.

"No."

"You weren't there. You don't know what it was like."

"I've been to other places, as you know full well. Stick to the plan, Mavis."

Mavis sighs, digs into her back pocket, pulls out three stapled wads of papers, and squats in front of the kneeling Johnson.

"No need to get all teared up. All you have to do is sign a document. In triplicate. We know what your signature looks like, so no cheating."

She thrusts the first wad into Johnson's nonplussed face.

"What —?"

"It's a legal document."

She crouches down, flicks her way through the wad, points at a space at the bottom of a page and provides a biro.

"To the best of my knowledge, all the events described in the preceding pages are accurate and truthful and can be supported by eyewitness accounts."

Warren says:

"I'd sign, if I were you."

Johnson scribbles a signature. Mavis looks at it, then up at Warren.

"It's the real McCoy."

Warren pretends to smile at Johnson.

"Good boy."

Mavis flicks through more pages and proffers another bottom page space.

"Another one here."

Johnson signs a second and then a third time. Janis hands the three sheaves to Warren.

"That's one for us, one for the lawyer…"

Johnson's face jerks upward.

"Lawyer?"

"*Solicitor*, beg pardon."

"And the third copy?"

"We're getting to that. Lie down."

"What?"

"My, you do look *worried*. On your back. You can get your suit dry-cleaned later."

"Now!"

Johnson hastens to obey. From the back of his belt Warren removes a hammer and hands it to Mavis.

"Thank-you."

Johnson raises his face.

"What are you -?"

Crouching, Mavis places a hand over Johnson's ankle then runs it a little way up the side of his leg.

"Looks about right."

She raises the hammer back over her shoulder and brings it down hard, just off Johnson's shin. A cracking sound. Johnson cries out.

"That's your fibula. It'll fix easily. We could have been nastier. We could have used a bat."

"Or kneecapped you," says Warren, his Beretta still trained on Jimbo.

"But a broken fibula'll stop you jumping, Jimbo; which'll give us time to call the police."

Mavis throws the third copy onto Johnson's supine chest.

"That's for them. Where d'you keep your car keys?"

Johnson taps a harlequined pocket. Mavis fishes them out and she and Warren head for the Jaguar. Their backs to Johnson, they pull off their balaclavas. Warren pockets his handgun and sticks the hammer back in his belt. Johnson can't get a clear view of their faces. All he can tell is, they're a lot younger than him. But (he can't help thinking, despite everything) not young enough *for* him.

XVI

Sarah looked up from the floor plan at Ralph and back again.

"You don't think you'll be spotted?"

Ralph sipped some coffee from a Snoopy mug.

"No. Once Janis's finished doing her stuff, my own mother wouldn't recognise me. Besides, everyone'll be rushing for the exit."

Janis leaned into the kitchen, hands gripping the doorframe:

"Get in here! Now!"

In the living-room, Mavis, wearing a different headscarf at the same angle as the last one, was adjusting the loop antenna on the little television set.

"Fucking thing...we had the image just a moment ago...There!"

Reginald Bosanquet appeared squarely and clearly, a mug shot of James Delaney posted just above his right shoulder.

"...the suspected ringleader of the armed terrorist gang known as The Vanguard was apprehended yesterday by police at his rented flat in Wellingford. An active member of the Real Workers' Party, Mr Delaney was caught red-handed with explosives of the type used in the most recent bombings for which The Vanguard have claimed responsibility..."

Pictures flashed up of two churches alight at night.

"…Mr Delaney claimed that he was working for MI5, a claim denied immediately by the security service."

Stevie raised a black fist:

"Yes!"

The others whooped and applauded. I watched in silence, astounded at seeing my handler accused of belonging to the very group that he'd tried to use me to trace.

"…With a key member of the gang under arrest and his materiel confiscated, a police spokesperson said that it was only a matter of time before the other members of the organisation were rounded up."

The news moved on. Sarah switched the set off and turned to the others. David said:

"Have to hand it to you, Stevie. That was very well done."

*

In the room lined with dark wood, the cockle-coloured eyes settle on James Delaney.

"What in God's name happened to you, Delaney?"

Delaney touches his sore cheekbone.

"Some policemen hit me, sir."

"I'm not bloody surprised. Now, I know, and you know – but fortunately nobody else knows – that you've been set up, though how you allowed that to happen to yourself, I haven't the faintest bloody idea."

"I'm so sorry, it was a –"

"Shut up. The point is, everybody else thinks you're a top banana in The Vanguard, and we want to keep it that way. From now on you will officially be at an undisclosed location so that Special Branch can interrogate you at length. Unofficially, you will also be in an undisclosed location, under the auspices of Five. You will be confined to a comfortable enough flat, and our chaps will make sure you do not so much as place your little toe beyond the threshold. Any questions?"

Delaney touches his cheekbone again. It hurts.

"How long would I be at this undisclosed location for, sir?"

"Until we actually do detain at least one real member of the Vanguard. And as we still don't have the first clue as to where they might be, that could take some time. There's a gentleman at the door who will escort you to your new abode. Begone."

XVII

As soon as Van walks up to the counter of Durham House, Doris presses the buzzer for the warden, thinking: *not this crazy blackie again.*

"Good afternoon."

"Afternoon."

"I've checked with my sister and she's adamant that her son, my nephew, was sent to Durham House. I wasn't mistaken."

Doris shakes her head, sighs, then glances up the corridor to see if there's any sign of the warden.

"I already told you, not only is your nephew not on file, but there are no boys of colour here. Not a one."

The warden approaches, wearing, as far as Van can see, the same jeans and jumper he had on a couple of days ago.

"Everything all right, Doris?"

"Well, not really. This gentleman's still insisting that his nephew's with us, and that's impossible, as we both know."

The warden turns a friendly face to Van.

"What makes you so convinced that your nephew is in Durham House, sir?"

Meanwhile, David squeezes himself into the basement through the same window he used two days ago and retrieves the Sennheiser bug that he had placed behind a pipe. As he squeezes himself out again, he can barely hear Van pretending to be obstreperous at the reception desk.

XVIII

Beth doesn't normally watch much TV at home, she's got one on all day at the pub, but back from work today, she doesn't feel tired, and there's an unpleasant itch in her mind that no amount of scratching will get rid of: the peculiar something that has happened to her boyfriend. So she sits with her fellow tenants as they argue about whether *This Is Your Life* is worth watching.

"It's old-fashioned shite," says one, "sort of thing my granny likes."

"Depends who the guest is", says another.

On the screen, Eamonn Andrews stands outside Broadcasting House, a big red book in hand.

"If he's standing outside the BBC, it'll be someone famous," says Beth.

The someone famous appears.

"Christ, not that old fart! Abort! Abort!"

"Leave it on," Beth says, "maybe he'll give us a recipe."

*

There are fifty or so people in the studio audience including Ralph, his hair greyed over, and a moustache glued believably to his upper lip. Not more than twenty yards from the front row, a stage has been furnished with red curtains and two opposing semi-circles of compact armchairs. The curtain parts and Eamonn Andrews steps onto the stage, clutching his big red book. Ralph and the rest of the audience applaud.

"Good evening everybody, and thank-you for coming to the show," says Eamonn, who can speak and smile at the same time. He glances at his watch. "And now it's time to present this week's mystery guest. A big hand, please, for Sebastian Hayley!"

Hayley steps through the curtains, wearing a pinstripe suit and a purple silk tie. His hair is slicked back, with a parting on one side.

"Welcome to *This Is Your Life*, Sebastian! You're looking very dapper today."

"Thank-you…"

Hayley gives a weasel-like grin as they shake hands.

"…well, you did accost me just as I'd finished recording a programme at the Beeb and these, as you know, are my working clothes."

Laughter from the audience. Eamonn Andrews indicates a seat at one end of the semi-circle of armchairs to his left.

"Please, take a seat…"

He opens the book.

"…there'll be some surprises for you coming up very soon, but for now we'd like to greet two people who you know very well, seeing them as you do most days of the week. Your wife Rosemary and your daughter, Cherie."

A middle-aged woman in evening dress and with an expensive looking necklace draped around her neck steps onto the stage together with a teenage girl of not more than fifteen, in teenage clothes. Applause. Hayley stands up and gives each of them a peck on the cheek.

"You knew about this, didn't you?"

"Of course, dear," replies the wife, "and I thought it was a wonderful idea. After all, you're hardly ever on the telly."

Laughter.

"Now there's one member of your family you see very rarely, because he lives a long way away. But we've flown him in from his home in Johannesburg. Your brother Tristram!"

Hayley shoots to his feet as a skinny man with a scraggly beard appears on the set. They give each other a brief hug.

"When was the last time you saw Sebastian?" asks Eamonn.

"Oh, quite a while. Before his hair went grey."

Laughter. A man in shadow off to the right puts down a card that reads LAUGHTER.

"Please take a seat, Tristram," and as Tristram does so, Eamonn Andrews turns to the audience, "Sebastian is almost as famous for his incredible command of languages as he is for his cooking. How many languages do you speak, Sebastian?"

Hayley makes play-it-down gestures with his hands.

"Oh, really, I don't like to boast –"

143

"Give us a rough idea!"

"About thirty."

"Thirty languages, ladies and gentlemen!"

The man in shadow cues the audience to clap. It does so.

"And today, we're going to meet a young lady who gave you classes in Armenian, one of the more difficult languages you've picked up."

Ralph leans forward, the better to catch Hayley's reaction.

"But I don't speak –" Hayley starts to say, but is cut off by Andrews who is already turning to where the curtain is parting to reveal Janis, dressed as a smart secretary, her hair in a bun, her shoes sensible, her skirt below the knee, her make-up making it hard for even Ralph to recognise her.

"Welcome, Lucine Vardanyan!" says Eamonn, "So how come such a lovely lady ended up giving Armenian classes to Britain's best-known chef?"

Janis smiles.

"Actually, I didn't. I claimed to be a naturalised Armenian-born woman in order to get on the show."

Eamonn Andrews is at a loss for words. Janis breaks the momentary silence:

"I'm here because when I was thirteen, this man…"

She points at Hayley.

"…raped me, on July the fifteenth, nineteen sixty-six. I was waiting for a bus here in London and this gentleman drove up and asked me if he could give me a lift. I recognised him on the spot, and, thrilled, I said yes. But he didn't take me home. He drove me out to the green belt. Epping Forest. He made me get out of the car, got out himself, unzipped his fly, made me kneel on the gravel and perform oral sex on him. He then raped me against his car, from behind. And I know there have been other victims. And I've also been reliably informed that he has a penchant for boys too."

Hayley roars:

"Nonsense! How in God's name? Nonsense! *Libellous* nonsense!"

Eamonn Andrews waves at someone in the wings.

"Cut transmission and call security!"

Ralph digs into his jacket pocket and pulls out the tip of a plumber's smoke grenade; he plucks a lighter from his other pocket and in the darkness that still shrouds the studio audience, he holds a flame to the touch paper, makes sure it takes, then removes it fully from his pocket and gently rolls it under the seats in front of him. After a moment, he stands up and shouts:

"Fire! There's a fire!"

Rolls of grey smoke are now uncoiling over the audience, which starts to hurry out of the seating area, accompanying itself with shouts of alarm. From the set, Eamonn Andrews calls:

"We've got a fire alert here! And where's security, for Christ's sake?"

The audience, Ralph included, is heading, higgledy-piggledy, for the exit door, now wide open, its sign brightly lit. The studio's sprinklers come on, soaking cameras, seats, the departing audience and Eamonn Andrews and Sebastian Hayley, whose wife and daughter and brother have not moved from their seats, staring at their husband and father and sibling as they are. Ralph follows the audience out through the exit door and into the main reception area, from which security guards are trying to make their way in the opposite direction, through to the studio, pushing panicky people out of their way. Ralph makes it out into the street's cold air. A block down, Janis is stepping into a taxi.

*

In the living room, Beth and her housemates have gone silent, staring heedlessly at the unexplained and unscheduled repeat episode of the Mary Tyler Moore Show that has come on seconds after Eamonn Andrews ordered the transmission to be cut.

The tattooed man says:

"What the fuck was that about?"

"I've heard the odd rumour about Hayley," says another.

"We all have," says the tattooed man, "But nothing as bad as what that girl said."

"She didn't look like she was making it up," says Beth, "and to judge from the priceless look on Eamonn Andrews's face, *he* believed her."

"Could have been a gimmick," says the tattooed man, "to get the ratings up."

Beth doesn't reply. Her memory's been niggled by a shot of the audience, panned over briefly when Hayley's wife made the joke about her husband not being on the telly much. There was a man in the third row who she's sure she's seen somewhere before. But where? When?

XIX

"Every major newspaper and every major radio station," David said, "has got a copy, with time, place and date clearly marked on the cassettes. The Sennheiser caught every scrap of sound. The journos'll be hearing Hugh Lowell MP, in that distinctive voice of his, telling that day's chosen boy what to do and everything that happens to that boy from then on."

We were back in the curtained South London living room.

Van said:

"That was three days ago, ample time for something to have appeared in the news. But no, not a dicky bird."

Janis said:

"And the only reaction to my exposure of Sebastian Hayley was the string of lies broadcast on LBC that same day, saying that the security guards had claimed that as I was running away I'd shouted at them – which I hadn't, obviously, they never even saw me – that I'd done the whole thing for a dare; then Haley made that statement saying he wouldn't be pressing charges, as this kind of practical joke was beneath his contempt. Christ, we even made him look good!"

Janis raises her copy of Jim Johnson's signed statement.

"Despite this, Jumping Jimbo is back on the small screen. Yet the police *must* have found the signed confession. And we sent a copy by courier to a lawyer. No action taken. Zilch."

Sarah said:

"So, no news in the news. Which is a pity, after all that work."

This was news to me.

"So your plan's *failed?* How could all the things you've done be kept so quiet?"

Sarah said:

"Somewhere up the line, somebody decided to let sleeping dogs lie through their teeth."

Ralph turned to me.

"We'd suspected something like this might happen. So it's straight on to plan B. Your professor Curtis is now the key, Lou."

"Our way in."

"Crucial."

"We'll blow them out of the water yet."

"Spill every last bean."

"If you're as ready and willing as you said you would be, then your time has come."

I thought I'd got over that first long shot of fear I'd felt when David and the others had shoved me into a car and driven

149

me off to an as yet unknown destination. But here it was again, suddenly unsettling my stomach, sprouting doubts.

"What, exactly, does this plan B consist of?"

PART FOUR: HELL FOR LEATHER

XX

David was looking uneasy as he walked past the seats of learning, as if their history was bearing down on him like a dead weight.

"I'm a soldier, not a fucking academic. What's my opening line again?"

"You need some help with your thesis about feminism in the work of William Godwin,"

"Of course," he said, "feminism. Godwin."

We walked under the arch of Wolverton College, its shadow further lowering the temperature of a chilly day.

"What brings you here, absentee?"

I ignored the porter's feigned astonishment.

"I believe Professor Curtis called you today to authorise a visit today from a postgraduate student over from Silverknee College," I nodded at David, "Benedict Cavendish. I'm here to make sure he knows where he's going."

The porter said:

"Yeah, I got that call."

He ran his finger down an open ledger on his sill.

"Here you are, Mr Cavendish. Got some ID? We can't be too careful, what with the Paddies up to their tricks day in and day out."

David handed over his passport, in which he looked younger than the slightly greyed thirty-something Janis had turned him into. The porter looked back and forth from the passport photo to David.

"Correct. You know where to take him, absentee?"

"I think I can still remember," I said in an attempt to be clever, and led David across a quadrangle, into another, smaller one.

"Who did the passport?"

"I could tell you that you're not on a need to know basis, but we're not in a fucking spy film. Van. He's an ace forger."

"Why that name? I mean, *Benedict Cavendish?*"

"He thought it sounded right for someone attending a posh university."

We entered a stairwell and went up one floor. I knocked on the oaken door I knew so well. Professor Curtis's voice – as friendly as ever – piped up:

"Come in!"

Curtis was sitting in his usual penumbra, crossed legs ending in his black lace-up Oxfords. He rose to his feet when David and I walked into his room.

"Professor, this is Benedict, the student I was telling you about."

"Ah, yes. Something about Godwin, what?"

"Feminism," said David, "in his work."

"Quite, quite. Please take a pew..." Curtis turned to me "...are you sitting in on this or would you prefer to –"

"Thank-you, but I'll leave the two of you to get on with it."

Curtis and David sat down, Curtis looking at David with a questioning expression. I left the room, closed the door, and placed my ear against it.

*

"Excuse me for asking," Curtis said in an unctuous voice that I hadn't heard him put on before, "but I can't help feeling that we've met somewhere before."

"You're right about that, professor. We've met, alright. Time and again. Many years ago."

Pause.

"I'm sorry, but I don't know what you're –"

"I was twelve. My name isn't Benedict Cavendish but you probably never caught my real one, any more than you did those of the other boys. For you, we were little more than interchangeable toys."

A short silence. Then Curtis half-sighed, half-groaned.

"Very well. No point in pretending. Or in playing the hypocrite. What is it you want from me? I could provide ample compensation, if that's what you –"

"It's not payment I want, Alan. Just one single favour. Or I tell everybody about you."

More silence.

"What kind of favour?"

Spoken in a voice so low I could barely hear it.

"I bear you no ill will, Alan. Since we last 'met', I've made progress. I'm rent now."

"Rent?"

"I work out of an open-air office in Piccadilly Circus."

"Ah."

"But the Dilly punters are a seedy, niggardly lot. Not a celebrity among them, unless you discount Jeremy Thorpe's occasional visits. So I'm seeking promotion, if you get my drift."

"I'm not sure I –"

"The grapevine has it that you're friends with Raymond Gibson."

"I'm sorry, I don't know –"

"Don't tell fibs, Alan. Gibson, says the grapevine, organises the most wonderful parties. Parties to which the great and the good are privy; including distinguished academics like your good self. The kind of party at which a not unattractive young lad could meet the right people."

"So you want –?"

"I want you to give Mr Gibson a bell and ask when the next party is. Or ask him to organise one. And get me an invite."

A longish pause.

"All right, tomorrow, I'll –"

"Right now, please."

"I don't know if he'll be –"

"If he isn't in, I'll wait here until he is. I work at night, so I've got all day."

The sound of a receiver being raised, a dial being fingered.

"It's me, Ray."

Curtis's side of the conversation was monosyllabic. At one point he interrupted it to speak to David.

"There's nothing until six weeks from now."

"Not good enough. Say you want a little get together within a fortnight."

And blow me if kind-hearted Alan Curtis didn't organise it there and then.

"Not this Saturday, the one after, at eight –"

"The address, Alan."

"The Oakhill Bed & Breakfast. Rectory Road, in Southwest London. A quiet street. Barnes, I believe, is the –"

"Fine. I take it you'll vouch for me when I turn up with you. I look forward to meeting a sample of the crème de la crème. Until then, *merci beaucoup et au revoir.*"

I stood to one side as David opened the door. We walked downstairs, across the quads and towards the exit.

"Didn't know you spoke French, David."

"I don't. Just those five words. Been rehearsing."

As we passed through the gate, the porter said:

"That was quick."

We ignored him. The sky, previously bleak enough, looked, when I glanced up at it, as if it was about to burst into tears.

XXI

Sir Michael and his number two, Sir Peter, are sipping brandies in the latter's new club. Pastel colours, bobbed or Bowie haircuts, velvet jackets, canned cool jazz, all customers under forty. Except for them.

"Didn't know your taste ran to such with-it places, Peter."

"I like things that swing," says Sir Peter, who is wearing a tight-fitting blue suit with slightly flared trousers. Sir Michael takes another sip.

"Why do you still want Five sniffing about on the edges of the Vanguard case, Peter? Why not just leave Special Branch to get on with it?"

"I asked your people to send a man in – what a pity it turned out to be that nincompoop Delaney – to try and find out as much as he could, because I had a hunch that The Vanguard was not the left-wing terrorist organisation it was making itself out to be. Special Branch has been following its usual protocols with respect to The Vanguard: raiding squats, that sort of thing. But my thinking is that the Vanguard aren't *really* interested in those symbolic actions using bombs and guns. That those actions were carried out (at least in part) so as to deliberately make the police think they are a far-left organisation, interested only in the so-called class struggle."

"So, in your view, what is it they *are* interested in?"

"Perhaps those VIPs whose peccadilloes we've just managed to sweep under the carpet?"

Sir Michael's cockle-coloured eyes widen.

"What makes you think that?"

"First off, the Vanguard has already claimed responsibility for the attacks on the premises where three of the aforementioned VIPs either lived and/or misbehaved."

"Misbehaved?"

"In a sexual manner."

"Oh."

"And now various attempts have been made, over the last few days, to name and shame those same people. We're currently examining the tapes of the This Is Your Life episode that was interrupted on live television. We believe that the woman who accused Hayley on air belongs to The Vanguard."

"Didn't she tell security at the TV station that she'd done it as a prank or something like that, before she ran off?"

"That was a story."

"Oh."

"And given that a plumber's grenade was found on the premises after all the kerfuffle, we also think she had an accomplice in the audience."

"So what do we do now, Peter? I confess I'm at a bit of a loss."

Sir Peter pauses.

"The information I'm picking up – I'm afraid I couldn't say how much is rumour and how much is fact – is that the Vanguard are preparing something we should be very concerned about."

"Rock a few boats, would it, this information?"

"*The* boat, Michael. I mean, we're talking about important men who have –"

Sir Michael raises his hand.

"Wiser to spare the details, Peter."

"Let's just say, then, that the situation is bad enough that if and when we locate the Vanguard, it may well be necessary to deploy SRRs."

Sir Michael puts down his glass.

"SRRs? Are you serious?"

"Very much so."

"All right, whatever you deem fit, Peter. Be so kind as to keep me in the loop."

"Of course, Michael, of course."

XXII

As soon as David and me got back and announced the date of the party which my former tutor had been coaxed into organising, the others got to work: in their bedroom, Ralph and Sarah started fiddling about with some sophisticated-looking pieces of electronic equipment that I couldn't identify, he sometimes with a jeweller's loupe scrunched into one eye; Mavis and Janis were poring over a large-scale street map in the kitchen; in the living-room, David and Warren were surrounded by a few of the orange slabs, pen-like sticks and thin metal pipes that I'd spotted some days ago in the broom cupboard upstairs.

"What are you doing?"

David looked up.

"We're making a bomb. Obviously."

On my way to my room I passed by Van's. He was crouched over his bedroom table surrounded by several glass jars full of different inks and a jumble of open passports, some newish, others dog-eared. He looked up.

"You're the only one I haven't got a picture of, Lou. You need to get on the Tube, take a longish journey, get into a photo booth, then come back on a different route. Change trains at least twice there and back."

I looked at the pile.

"Why would I need a new passport?"

He shrugged.

"Maybe you don't. It's just in case."

I hesitated.

"Can I ask you something?"

"Why I'm involved in all this, even though I'm not a victim of abuse?"

He looked up, smiling.

"That's…right."

Van explained he had been born in Jamaica but had been sent with an aunt to England when he was two. At age three, when waiting at a bus stop with that same aunt, a white woman had spat on his head, which was the opening gambit in a series of deeds done by racist English people from all walks of life, designed to make him feel humiliated, humble, unwanted, displaced, hated. At school, when looking for work, when walking along the street: words, punches, threats, two assaults, five unwarranted arrests.

As for Stevie, he added, she had been born here, but had been through much the same. And worse. When she was twenty, four white men pulled her into a doorway and insulted her skin even as they groped it, and would have gone further if a passing group of (white) women hadn't screamed at them to stop.

Van had said:

"Me, I just want to see the gentlemen at the top shown up for what they are. Then, hopefully, people will change their attitudes towards them and, even more hopefully, throw their hatred of dark skin in the bin, when they see that we aren't any worse than some of the most decorated, most prestigious, most untouchable paleskins in the country; that we might even be somewhat better. On top of all of which..." he gestured around him, "these people are friends of mine."

*

When I got back from a photobooth in distant Stoke Newington, I handed him the set of four identical mugshots, and went to lie down. I was missing Beth. Stretched out on the bed, staring at the dusty lace curtains, I felt an ache of desire, a yearning.

What was she doing now? What was she thinking about my unannounced disappearance? Was she now convinced I was one of those men who just up and leave without a word of warning: a snake, a louse, a toe rag, a scumbag?

I wondered what she'd make of the people I was with. I wondered about them myself sometimes, not least because so far they'd declined to tell me the details of their current 'plan B'.

*

After a week had gone by, there was a knock on my door. Ralph stuck his head into the room.

"We're ready."

I followed him downstairs into the living room. The kitchen table had been placed in the middle and the whole group was sitting around it, studying Mavis and Janis's large-scale map.

Then Ralph, Sarah and David ran us through the plan, step by step, task by task.

Afterwards there were a few questions, then Van went upstairs and came back with a wad of passports, some newish, others dog-eared. He handed each one to its designated owner, myself included.

"There you go. Like I said, just in case."

I opened it and looked, astonished, at a stamped picture of myself next to a name I'd never heard of before.

Stevie got up, went into the kitchen, and came back with a bottle of whisky.

"I think we could all do with a drop of this."

It was the first time I'd seen any alcohol on the premises. And yes, I for one needed a drop. Or ten.

XXIII

Delaney gets up and opens his bedroom door. A young man in black suit, white shirt, black tie, and with a short (but not a military) haircut, looks up from a Formica table.

"Morning, sir."

"There's no need to call me 'sir' all the time."

"I'm a trainee officer, sir. You outrank me."

"Outrank you though I might, you're still doing a pretty good job of keeping me cooped up in this poxy little flat."

"I'm under orders, sir."

"I guess I'll have my umpteenth cup of tea."

"Would you like me to make it for you, sir?"

"No, thank-you, I'm quite capable of plugging in a kettle and dropping a bag of Typhoo into a mug."

"As you wish, sir."

Delaney walks around the table to where the cooker sits, and makes his tea.

"I'm going to sit in the living-room, if that's OK by you."

"You're free to move around the flat, sir."

"I wouldn't mind being on my own for a little while."

"I'll stay where I am then, sir."

Delaney walks into the living room, flicks on the small black and white TV, and plonks himself down on the sofa. He sighs: here, in this small flat, he is becoming claustrophobic.

A football match jiggles about on the screen, men in shirts and shorts running, stopping, kicking, tackling. What, Delaney asks himself, am I watching this for? I've never been interested in football, I've never given a flying fuck who wins what cup.

The walls move an inch or two closer in.

XXIV

Beth watches the soundless TV screen, her hands dunking glasses automatically into a revolving washer. A wildlife programme. Anything to stop her thinking about her vanished boyfriend. A section about mating otters finishes, and one about lions hunting appears. The lions are stalking a zebra, making it look like they're going to take their time, until one of them suddenly leaps up and brings the zebra down and the other lions move in, tearing the still-living striped horse apart, white and black stomach spilling intestines, bubble eyes a-goggle, limbs kicking air.

Surprised, horrified, Beth drops the next glass due to be dunked. When it shatters, the landlord turns his head.

"What the hell is wrong with you? For the last few days, you've been forgetting prices, giving the wrong change. And this isn't the first broken glass, either."

Without looking at him, she starts to sweep up the slivers.

"I'm stressed."

"What about?"

She brushes the slivers into a dustpan.

"It's personal."

She tips the slivers into the bin.

"Personal or not, I need a barmaid who knows what she's doing. You go on like this, I'll have to let you go."

She looks at him.

"Really?"

Before he (open-necked white shirt, late forties, stocky, shorter than he'd like to be) can say anything, a woman appears at the bar and orders a pint of Holsten. Beth takes a clean glass, tips it under the tap and recalls that this was the make of lager that her boyfriend had ordered what seems like half a century ago, when he was just a stranger who'd asked her to turn up the volume on the TV. To see the news... As the liquid splashes gently into the glass, her memory gets the jog she's been itching for: the man in the third row of *This Is Your Life* is, without a doubt despite his older looks, the man who was earlier reported missing: her boyfriend's friend.

She serves the lager, gives the right price and returns the right change. The name follows, in a rush. Finns. Ralph Finns. Whose Dad, according to the Mirror she'd shown her boyfriend, when Ralph Finns was apparently missing no longer, was a 'scrap metal mogul'.

There are no more customers on the horizon. She goes into the back, comes out with the Yellow Pages, and opens it up on the bar. It takes her a couple of minutes to find

FINNS METAL RECYCLING LTD.

She lifts the bar flap and goes to the payphone.

"Phoning on the job again are we, Beth?"

"Won't be long."

She asks the company's receptionist if she could talk to Mr Finns.

"Mr Finns?"

"Yes, Mr Finns, the proprietor, if I'm not mistaken, of Finns Metal Recycling Ltd."

"Is this a business matter?"

"No, it's personal."

The receptionist actually sniggers.

"I'm sorry, but Mr Finns does not take personal calls at the office."

"So where does he take them?"

"If it's a personal call, you should know his home number."

"Well, I don't. Could you give it to me, please?"

"I'm afraid I'm not authorised to do that."

Click. Beth rips the page out of the guide.

"Hoi! What do you think you're doing?"

Beth looks at her boss.

"Let me go. Just for one day."

XXV

A middle-aged woman with a Yoko-Ono-ish hedge of hair that wobbled on her skull walked down the stoop of Oakhill Bed & Breakfast and stepped into a Mini parked under a lemon-squeeze of light from a nearby lamp-post. From the dark end of Rectory Road, Mavis and I watched her drive off. I checked my watch. Nine on the dot. We'd pulled straws to see who would keep this house under surveillance and when. Mine and Mavis's was the last shift. I felt good. I was certain that Beth would approve, might even applaud, might even be a mite proud of me, because this wasn't to do with politics, which I knew she'd written off as a mug's game, but this was something else entirely.

The woman we'd been watching was the sole owner of the B&B. We didn't know her name. Her guests this evening: a male couple, a female couple, and a man with two women. Mavis, headscarfed as ever, muttered:

"Clocks off at nine sharp and leaves her guests to their own vices."

"So it seems."

She squinted at me.

"Does it shock you?"

"No, but I don't understand why people need to use a bed and breakfast. It isn't illegal to be gay. It isn't illegal to sleep with more than one person."

Mavis gave a snort.

"One of the two men and one of the two women are probably married with kids. As for the trio, those women were much younger than the john. Prostitutes. Or fools."

Our shift over, we started to walk away from Rectory Road. Mavis seemed tense. I said:

"Not that I'm an expert, but there must be ways of having sex without being furtive."

"Some people enjoy it more when it's furtive. Some people..."

Her voice pitched up.

"...enjoy it more when it's illegal."

"I'm sorry, Mavis, I didn't mean to —"

She tapped my arm.

"You needn't worry about bringing back any memories of mine, because they're always there, and they always will be..."

A thin crack in her voice.

"...because I'll never never never be able to understand how grown men can bring themselves to even *think* of doing those things, let alone *doing* them, let alone repeating them again and again and again. Those of us who've allowed ourselves to have such things done to us have been put for good behind the bars of our memories, where all we can do is wonder about how such things are not only possible but why they happened to us. Why *us?*"

She was looking at me as if she expected me to answer. I shook my head.

"Then I'll tell you. Because we were easy pickings, kids from approved schools or hostels or runaways. We were easy to round up, easy to be mickey-finned and plied with liquor, easy to abuse. But what I don't see is what did those gentlemen get out of it, really? Was it *really* so much nicer to fuck a child than to fuck an adult? Did their privileged members *really* get more of a thrill when the hole penetrated belonged to someone too young to understand what was happening? And even if their members did get more of a thrill, was that enough to justify ruining so many people's lives? Couldn't they have gone elsewhere, used prostitutes, masturbation, melons? These questions go round and round in my head each and every day; each and every day I hear their orders spoken as casually as if they were ordering a drink, their grunts of pleasure that crushed my childhood self, that stubbed it out. Before I joined the group, I was less than a nobody, and I was drinking to keep it that way; suicide was a permanent option, something to look forward to if and when the drink failed to do its job."

She stopped talking. The only thing that occurred to me to say was:

"How did you come across the others?"

"One of them happened to be sitting opposite me on the same bus. She saw the tears running down my cheeks, something they often did without warning, and she came up and asked if I needed any help and I said what kind of fucking help are *you* going to give *me?* After all, I'd been in and out of therapy for years and a fat lot of good it'd done me. But she –"

"Janis?"

"Janis asked me to come and meet some friends of hers and she said it in a way which didn't sound patronising, didn't sound pitiful, didn't sound like she was making herself feel good by doing a stranger a favour. And once I'd met her friends, once I'd heard what they intended to do, that put an end to my tears for good."

She checked her watch.

"We're done. We've confirmed the owner doesn't live on the premises. We know from the others that she goes back to her B&B around about midday to tidy up after her guests have gone. She doesn't employ a cleaning lady: I imagine the owner doesn't want anyone finding the used condoms, or nipple clamps and butt plugs or whatever else it is the guests use to squeeze some pleasure out of each other. But that means the place is only empty for a part of the morning, between the last guests' departure in the small hours and the landlady's midday arrival. That means Robert and David'll have to go in in broad daylight, when the street might be busy. And shit, I almost forgot…"

She pointed.

"…there's your phone box. Walk to it fast but not so fast you might attract attention. I'll time you."

XXVI

Beth gets off the train at King's Cross and makes her way to the Sydenham address on her torn off Yellow Page. A warehouse next to an esplanade containing twin heaps, almost hills, of glistening metal scraps.

On her way, she's thought about why she is doing this, about the hold her boyfriend has on her, that has made her leave her place of work and come all this way, just on a hunch that her boyfriend's disappearance and Ralph Finn's presence in the *This Is Your Life* audience are connected, somehow.

Love happens when you least expect it, she thinks, and it may well be a need, perhaps even an addiction: a longing for something you sometimes get fed up with but can never get enough of.

The warehouse door is open. She walks into a large, poorly lit space on which stand pincer cranes that remind her of the glassed-in miniature ones poised over gee-gaws in amusement arcades. A metal staircase leads up to an office in which several people lit by fluorescent tubes are working at their desks. She goes up, knocks and walks in. Heads rise and a woman asks her where she's going. Beth doesn't answer, having already spotted the door marked

JEFFREY FINNS, MANAGING DIRECTOR

to which she walks over, knocks twice and goes in without waiting for a response, to find the man she saw in the newspaper looking up from a large mahogany desk.

"Mr Finns?"

"That's what it says on the door."

That London accent.

"Do you know your son's been on the telly? Recently?"

He puts down his pen. The woman who asked her where she was going, appears at the door.

"I'm sorry, Mr Finns, she just came barging through –"

Finns raises a hand.

"No worries."

The secretary leaves. Jeffrey Finns turns back to Beth.

"Ralph was in the news *fairly* recently, yes. And who are you?"

"I'm a friend of a friend of Ralph's. Beth."

"Take a seat, Beth…"

She takes one of the two facing him. He looks at her, a crease of curiosity on an otherwise staid face.

"…and tell me what's on your mind."

"My friend's gone missing, and I think there's a possibility he could be with Ralph. They knew each other well."

"Ralph's on his honeymoon. I don't think he'd appreciate any extra company."

"The last time I saw Ralph he was in a Thames Television studio. In London. A week ago."

Jeffrey Finns' eyes widen a touch.

"You've got to be mistaken, Beth."

"According to what it said in the paper, you're funding him at the moment. And to do that, you need to know where he is. I just want to check if my friend's with Ralph or not. That's all."

He stares at his blotter for a moment, then looks up.

"I'll tell you exactly what I know and what I don't. Every two months, I send a sum of cash to a post office box number here in London, because my son prefers cash to a money order or a check or a wire transfer. Nor have I taken the trouble to find out the precise location of the PO Box, because I don't want my son to think I'm trying to spy on him. Besides, I doubt very much he picks up the money in person: someone else probably does it for him and sends it to wherever he happens to be. But like I said, I don't think he would have joined a TV audience. Which programme was it?"

"*This Is Your Life.*"

Finns chuckles.

"He *hates* that show. So there you go. Now, I could give you the box number and you could waste I don't know how much time finding out where it is and far more time hanging around the post office trying to see if anybody opens that particular box. But I'm not going to give you the number. I don't want my son or any of his helpers being followed around. My son has a right to his privacy."

"Why do you give him all this money, if you don't even know where he is?"

"Personal reasons. And now I'm going to have to ask you to leave. When my son gets back from his honeymoon, you can ask him to his face if he knows anything about your friend."

Beth stands up.

"I'm obviously not getting anywhere here."

She opens his door.

"I'm sorry I couldn't be of more help, Beth. Now, now, no need to turn on the waterworks."

XXVII

"And how long are *you* going to be with me?"

Delaney's once bloated face has thinned out, his slim body has grown skinny, his usual black clothes look as if they've been slept in – because they have – and his smooth skin has a faint tint of grey. He is talking to his new minder, who, like the last one, is wearing a black suit and tie and a white shirt; and unlike the last one can't be much over twenty and therefore, perhaps, easier to convince.

"We rotate on a weekly basis, sir."

Delaney sits down at the Formica table in the little kitchen, opposite the officer.

"What's your name? Your first name, I mean?"

"Derrick, sir."

"Look Derrick, I won't beat about the bush: being in here twenty-four hours a day isn't good for my health, physical or mental. I need a breath of fresh air, even if it's just for five or ten minutes. I'd stick close to you, there'd be no danger of me doing a runner. Not that I want to do one. We could see the sights of

Bromley. Its coin-op, its kebab take-away, its corner shop run by a tired looking Pakistani."

"I'm sorry, sir, but I can't do that. I'm under orders."

Delaney slams his hand palm down on the Formica.

"I know you're under orders! You all say the same bloody thing! I'm not asking you to disobey your orders, I'm asking you to release me from this bloody suburban cage for a little while! Is that too much to ask?"

"I've been given very specific instructions, sir. And they do not include allowing you out of the flat."

This time, it's Delaney's *fist* that slams down on the table.

"For fuck's sake!"

He gets up, strides into his bedroom, lies down, suppresses a moan, and tries to get some shut-eye. In vain.

XXVIII

Party time!

I woke up early, smelling the dust in my room, the plaster on the edges of the ceiling, the damp on the wallpaper. I got slowly out of bed, washed at my washbasin, looked out at the street through the net curtain, then got dressed. Flared jeans, Kickers, a cheesecloth shirt. I went downstairs and was surprised to find everyone was already down there, sipping tea or coffee. And smoking. Van looked up.

"All right?"

"Bit nervous."

"Aren't we all?"

*

Yesterday, just before twelve, Ralph and David had come back from the B&B on Rectory Road, their mission accomplished.

They were all set now: Ralph, Mavis, Janis, Warren, Van, David and Stevie. Sarah was pulling on her biker's jacket.

Warren called out:

"On our way!"

Mine was going to be a lonely, circuitous route, like everyone else's. I pulled on an anorak and stepped into the twilight, the houses now half black and half purple, the air smelling of moist paving and scraps of rubbish. I walked five blocks to the bus stop I'd been assigned. There were three other passengers waiting: a white man in his thirties, and two middle-aged black women. The bus rolled round the corner and halted at the stop. We all got on and it was only when I clambered up the stairs to the top deck, bright as a public convenience, that I started to worry that the other passengers would notice how nervous I was. Or smell my profusely sweating armpits.

I watched the people walking along the pavements below me, all sizes, all kinds of clothes, all ages, both sexes, both directions. The vehicles that passed the bus, changing lanes, looked like so many bumper cars. My God, I thought, if any of those people down there knew what we were about to do.

I counted five stops and got off. Tottenham Court Road. All the shops chock full of electronic gadgets except for Ann Summers, its window showing off tight lingerie, split-crotch panties, slim vibrators. I made my way to the Tube station entrance, trotted down the stairs, bought a ticket and took the escalator down past rectangular photos of women in bras. Four people along stood the white man who'd been in the original bus queue. My heart felt like it had been punched. Not for the first time, I wondered – if only for an instant – if I was really cut out for this sort of thing.

Then the man got into the carriage next to mine.

But got off at the next stop. I shook my head at my own jitteriness, before getting off myself at Highgate and making my way to Makepeace Avenue. There were no shops or services in this part of town, just a long row of tomb-silent semi-detached houses. I walked along the pavement, avoiding the pools of lamplight.

Ralph had clued me in that very morning:

"It's a discontinued model, an LDV Pilot, second-hand, picked it up for a song. We just have to hope the cops don't stop us on the way, but then again, why would they stop a television detector van?"

"It's a detector van?"

"Why d'you think I got it for next to nothing? There was nothing in it, of course, those things are there to scare people into paying their licence."

"Seriously?"

"Of course."

"And you fixed it up in broad daylight?"

"Did the work in a hired garage out in Highgate."

And there that garage was now, right where he'd said it would be, at number thirteen, its metal door open a third of the way. I bent down and went in, bumping my spine against the blind. Inside, I could barely make out the black lump of a vehicle. I was half way over when the cabin light was switched on, revealing Janis and Warren, she at the wheel, he in the passenger seat. The vehicle, I saw when I approached, was a gunmetal grey van with what looked like a small radar perched on its roof and the words 'TELEVISION DETECTOR' painted along its side. Warren wound down the passenger window, stuck his head out, and gave me a hissy whisper.

"What took you so long? Pull the garage door up and get in the back."

I went back to the entrance, put my hands under the bottom edge of the door and pushed upwards. It didn't budge. I tried a few more times.

"It's stuck."

The driver's door opened and Janis got out.

"What's the matter, didn't eat your spinach?"

She came over to the door and shoved it up hard.

"Get in the back."

The van's back doors were flung open. I climbed in.

"Oh, wow."

A faint light had been fitted to the ceiling of the windowless body of the van. Ralph and Sarah were seated at two small stools in front of a console with dials and a couple of volume unit meters, on top of which sat a small monitor, an even smaller speaker and a video cassette recorder. The space was full to bursting, what with the two at the console plus Mavis and Van and Stevie and me, all of us standing. Stevie pulled the doors shut. Mavis (minus her headscarf) and Stevie were dressed up in smart skirts and natty jackets. Van, pretty smart himself in a beige leather jacket and cotton slacks, was watching Sarah as she fiddled with the speaker. After a few seconds it clicked and whirred.

"We're on."

Ralph glanced at her.

"Take it down a bit…"

She adjusted a dial and the sound level on the VHS recorder hopped out of the red.

"Let's go."

Ralph spoke with the quiet authority he'd shown behind the scenes during school productions, when he was in control of the lighting and the sound and the backdrop. And here he was now, crouched over this assemblage of his own making: Ralph, my more-or-less-friend, Ralph, this time with no bottle of fine wine at his side, just him, in an old T-shirt, turning dials and flicking switches.

Van slapped twice on the window that gave onto the driver's cabin. Janis switched on the ignition and drove the vehicle slowly out of the garage. Stevie said:

"It's kind of fuggy in here. Someone forgot to put on their deodorant."

That might have been me.

"Why don't you take your jacket off, Alice? You must be boiling."

Sarah shook her head.

"I'm fine."

The journey to Rectory Road took just over an hour, Janis driving carefully but even so, as the stools weren't fixed, Sarah and Ralph found themselves gripping the edge of the console so as not to fall off, and the rest of us had to lean against the side of the van to stay on two feet. When we came to a full stop, the motor still running, Warren slid back the connecting window.

"We're in Ranelagh Avenue, on the corner of Rectory. Want to see if you can pick up the signal?"

Ralph stood up, checked the monitor's connections and switched on. Grey snow. He sat back down and flicked a switch on the console. An indecipherable image began to materialise on the monitor screen. He turned a dial, slowly. The image became a touch more solid.

"Can't we park a little closer?"

The van swung gradually round a corner and advanced a few yards.

"We're now in Rectory Road itself, about seven houses down from the B&B."

Ralph reached for the dial again. This time a clear enough fish-eye image of an empty living room came into view, in which there were a couple of lit standing lamps, several studded leather armchairs and two sofas ditto, as well as a long coffee table in the centre. We were now staring at the screen like dogs at a stranger.

Ralph murmured:

"Took David and me a while to get that camera installed."

"But there's no sound. Is there?"

"David's wearing a mike. We'll get sound as soon as your tutor brings him along."

Sarah glanced at her watch:

"How come they've already put all the lights on? The party isn't supposed to begin for another hour."

Mavis pointed:

"Because of him, probably."

A man in a black suit and tie had entered the room, cradling two ice buckets. He placed them on the coffee table and went out again. Ralph pressed the record button on the VCR.

"Who *is* that?"

Sarah shook her head.

"We don't have that gentleman clocked."

Stevie said:

"The guests aren't the sort of people who bring along their own drinks and nibbles, are they? Must be some kind of waiter."

The man reappeared several more times, first with more ice buckets, then with bottles of champagne to put in them, then with flute glasses, which he set out in two rows on the coffee table.

Ralph knocked on the glass of the driver's cabin.

"Hey Warren, time for you to take a cigarette break. And for some of the others to take their strolls."

Janis doused the headlights, killed the motor and stepped out of the vehicle. Warren stayed in the passenger seat and lit a Woodbine. Stevie opened the van's back doors and peeked left and right:

"Let's get going."

Ralph said:

"Spot any cops, let us know."

"We know the drill, Rob."

Van joined her and the two of them strolled around the block, off to our left. Then Mavis got out and she and Janis headed over to our right.

Inside, Ralph was trying to sharpen the image. His forehead was shiny with sweat. I looked at my watch.

"It's time."

The speaker crackled into life and we heard a muffled ding-dong and after a few seconds, the lounge door opened and the man in the black suit ushered David and Curtis in. David was in a pressed brown, wide-lapelled jacket and a dark polo-neck sweater. Curtis turned to the waiter:

"Thank-you, Jeeves."

"Jeeves?"

Ralph looked round at me.

"All these people use false names. Just in case. Even the minions."

"Just like us!"

Sarah tutted while fiddling with the sound controls.

"No, Lou, not like us. Watch."

'Jeeves' said:

"The champagne should be chilled by now."

"Splendid, Jeeves. We shall serve ourselves."

"Very good, sir."

'Jeeves' closed the lounge door after him. David looked around.

"So this is the romper room, is it?"

"Please, take a seat."

David sat down in one of the armchairs. Curtis took a chair opposite.

"Champagne?"

"Why not?"

Curtis pulled one of the bottles out of the nearest bucket, shook it, then popped the cork. Foam splashed out.

"Whoa, Alan, you'll soak the carpet!"

Curtis placed two glasses in front of him and filled them to overflowing.

"Here, my good man, we can do absolutely as we wish. Normal rules do not apply."

He handed a glass to David, who took a small sip. Silence. Curtis raised his.

"Bottoms up, as it were."

He let out a chuckle short as a fart. David raised his, a mite.

"Cheers, Alan."

Their glasses clicked instead of clinking.

"Plastic flutes, professor? I thought this was a high-class affair."

Curtis said:

"Glass can break. Which could make things messy."

The doorbell. Ushered into the room moments later was a person we all knew well enough.

Curtis stood up.

"Why, if it isn't old Lizzy!"

He shook Sebastian Hayley's hand.

"Lizzy?"

"Hayley's a TV chef, so they call him after Elizabeth David, the cookery writer. I told you, they've all got these ever so clever nicknames."

"Allow me to introduce you to an old friend of mine; Dave, say hello to Lizzy," said Curtis, as David waggled his fingers by way of a hello.

"Splendid," said Hayley, "and what do you do, young man?"

"That depends," said David.

"Good answer, sir!"

Hayley poured himself a drink and sat down at the far end of the room, the back of his head just visible to the camera. More rings at the door. One by one, familiar faces were shown into the room by 'Jeeves': Hugh Lowell MP, addressed by the others as Rake; children's TV presenter Jimbo Johnson, aka Bubbles. Banter with an excited edge to it was ping-ponged back and forth, except by David, who limited himself to smiling at the other's jokes.

Then a man I didn't recognise appeared, wearing a velvet suit and pointy shoes. He went around shaking everybody's hand. When he came to David, he said:

"Ah, and who might this be?"

My tutor smiled:

"Someone who will be more than happy to take part in the festivities."

"Excellent," he said, "always good to have an older lad on hand. How are we off for champers?"

"Fine, fine, Mister Twisty!" they chorused in broken unison.

"Who's that?"

"That bastard," said Sarah, "is Raymond Gibson. The fixer. "

Ralph pointed at the screen.

"Curtis, Hayley, Johnson, Lowell and Gibson make five."

The chit-chat was getting a touch more raucous, interspersed now with the odd guffaw, the odd loud cackle. People were leaning forward in their seats at regular intervals to pour themselves some more. David did the same. He looked as if he needed it.

Ding-dong!

Another man entered and this time the prattling ceased and everyone stood up. In his late forties, he was wearing a tight-fitting blue suit with slightly flared trousers, and carrying a briefcase as big as a Gladstone bag. Sarah's jaw dropped:

"Fuck."

The newcomer took one of the armchairs and placed the briefcase next to it, on the floor.

"You're looking well, Namyal," said Lowell, "how's 'retirement' treating you?"

Slight chuckles all round. I said:

"Namyal?"

Ralph said:

"His name spelt backwards. I'm telling you, it's an effort to keep up with these people."

"Retirement," said Namyal to the others in that outsize lounge, "is proving to be most interesting. But of course I can't tell you much about it. Nothing at all, in fact."

His thickish lips smiled.

"Damn it, Namyal, not even a titbit?"

"Absolutely not."

Jimbo Johnson nodded at the briefcase:

"You shouldn't be mixing business with pleasure, old chap."

"There are some things, my dear Bubbles, which I simply have to have close to me."

The man they called Mr Twisty – Raymond Gibson, the fixer – checked the time:

"The evening's entertainment will be here shortly. Fresh bunnies. All the way from Rake's stamping ground."

Hugh Lowell, MP, gave a faux bow from his seat to a round of gentle applause. More chuckles.

"Who *is* Namyal?"

Sarah humphed.

"A former civil servant. Assigned to the Ministry of Defence, then to the Foreign Office. And now – and that's why they're all making these sly comments about his retirement – he's currently working as an informal intelligence operative. Like your handler, Lou, only much, much higher up."

Ralph said:

"Sir Peter Layman, knight of the realm."

Layman had a glass in one hand and a recently lit cigar in the other, which, as he spoke, he jabbed in the direction now of one guest, now of another.

"We all know there are people who wouldn't approve of our evening's entertainment, people who would lock the lot of us up, if they could. And for what? For what, hey? Just for giving younger people the same pleasure we're taking from them. Yet there are murderers who get shorter sentences than we would. It's ridiculous."

The others mumbled 'hear, hear.'

"Scandalous!"

That was Jimbo Johnson. I looked at David. He was downing a whole flute in one go, unnoticed by the others. As he was putting his glass down, Layman turned to him, unexpectedly.

"Who's the fetching lad here?"

Curtis said:

"Dave. An acquaintance of mine."

Layman focussed on David across the tip of his raised nose.

"Well, Dave, what do *you* think about all this?"

David shifted in his chair, and coughed.

"I reckon it's all right for people to do as they please, as long as everyone is in agreement to do it."

"Splendid," roared Layman, "Splendid! Somebody pour this chappy a drink!"

Curtis picked up an open bottle and filled David's glass. A phone rang, somewhere outside the room. Raymond Gibson stood up.

"Excuse me, gentlemen."

He left the room, leaving the door ajar. Hayley rubbed his hands.

"Wonder what he's got for us this time, ay?"

I watched Hugh Lowell MP's arm reach out for more bottle.

"Something rather special, so I've been told."

"Ooh," said Jimbo Johnson, "inside information."

"That's more my line of business," said Layman in a flat voice, "but I confess I haven't got a clue. I'd supposed it would be the usual fare."

Laughter, though not from David. Hugh Lowell shook his head.

"No, no. Something different tonight. You'll see."

"Whatever," said Layman, "same rules apply: this simply should not be illegal. Not for nothing do they say the law is an ass."

A pause. Then Curtis, my tutor, broke in:

"I can't agree."

Lowell's brillantined head turned to him.

"Why ever not, Dolly?"

I tapped Ralph on the shoulder.

"What's the origin of 'Dolly'?"

Without taking his eyes off the monitor, Ralph said:

"We never got around to working that one out."

Curtis was sitting up ramrod straight.

"I accept that I cannot help but be attracted to younger people…"

He made a whishing sound, as if shooing his last words away.

"…but I'm being euphemistic, it is to *children* I have always been attracted. This attraction is something I have not been able to help and which I have felt strongly since adolescence, when it was nothing but a source of shame, something I desperately tried to keep under wraps, from my parents, my friends, from *the world*. It was only when I was in my twenties that I discovered there were other people who had the same proclivities as myself, that I was not alone and what was more, that if I took the same precautions as they did, I could satisfy my needs. At first, I contacted male prostitutes through magazines on an individual basis, boys of fifteen, fourteen, perhaps even younger, I didn't ask. I did not feel any remorse at the time, after all, their services were on offer and I paid the agreed price, thus convincing myself that these transactions were consensual. But when I got talking to these lads, those who were willing to talk, I found out what should have been obvious to me, namely that they were working for adults – pimps – who told them where to go and then took a percentage of the proceeds. These boys often lived in hostels run by these same procurers, who abused them at will and kept a close eye on their charges, who were often badly fed and kept strictly on the premises except when released to service a client. One day, I was approached in my college rooms by another Fellow – I was a mere Fellow then, too – who told me he'd heard about what he called my *interests*. He introduced me to an organised circle of like-minded people, both in and outside the university, and, in some cases, from outside the town, who paid a little bit more for cleaner, younger boys who – rather than being kept locked up in insalubrious hostels – lived in approved homes and charitable orphanages. And it was through the men in this circle that I finally came into contact – I was by this time a Regius Professor – with the distinguished company in which I find myself today…"

He said it without irony and with a pencil-thin smile.

"…I told myself that I should stop, that enough was enough, that what I was doing was not right. But my impulses got the better of me every time, until my conscience was reduced to little more than a tiny voice, whining pathetically somewhere deep down in here…"

He pointed at the side of his head.

"…despite which, I remain aware that I am not doing any favour to the boys with whom I couple. They are not doing this of their own free will. And I suspect that their later lives may well be seriously affected by such activities. But I do not wish to be hypocritical. I fully admit that I am unable to alter my preferences, or to stifle my desires."

He immediately took a long swig. Sir Peter Layman went:

"Got that off your chest have you, Dolly?

Curtis nodded.

"I suppose I have."

At that moment, Gibson slipped back into the room.

"Then I do believe it's time for the revelry to begin. Mr Twisty, how fares our fare?"

Gibson smiled.

"Our fare is now ready and waiting. Shall I serve them up for your delectation?"

"If you would be so kind," Layman grunted.

Gibson hurried back out. The room fell silent. Professor Curtis scratched his ear. Jimbo took a sip and smacked his lips, audibly. Layman cradled his chin in one hand and chef Hayley tapped his fingers against the right arm of his chair. David quickly downed another glass.

*

Ralph turned to me:

"Set to go, Lou?"

"All set."

Sarah said:

"Got enough change?"

I dug my hands into my pockets and pulled out what coins were there. No fifty pees, no twenties, no tens even.

"Fuck."

Both Sarah and Ralph swivelled round and stared at me.

"Lou, are you seriously telling me you didn't bring enough change?"

"It just didn't…"

"Occur to you," finished Sarah.

"What about you? Have you got anything?"

Sarah fished out a coin.

"Ten pee. Not enough."

Ralph shook his head.

"Fuck, Lou, we *talked* about this."

"I'm sorry…"

"Fuck being sorry!" He turned to Sarah. "What now?"

"Lou, get out and find one of the two pairs of lookouts. And let's hope, for your sake, that they happen to have a few coins on them."

I pulled the door open, and stepped out of the van's fug into Rectory Road, made chilly by a breeze blowing off Putney Common. I turned left into Ranelagh Avenue and then left again into Elm Grove Road. It was empty. I started walking up it, breaking into the occasional jog. I was a third of the way to the end when Mavis and Janis hoved into sight, holding hands.

*

Once they'd handed me enough change, I ran back to the van as fast as I could.

"It's OK," I said, forgetting to keep my voice down to a stage whisper, "I got the change!"

Ralph and Sarah didn't budge an inch, didn't so much as flinch in my direction. They were staring at the monitor, their empty mouths making slow chewing motions.

XXIX

Beth leans on the bar, looking at the sparsely populated interior of the pub, wondering how her boss – idle to her left – could be so inept as to allow his place to be all but empty on a Saturday evening. How has he managed that in a town where the entire population floods to the pubs on this day of the week? She would have taken measures: a pool table maybe, or a better jukebox, some food, or at the very least some snacks that beat crisps and pork scratchings.

A weasel clambers up Beth's spine, tickling, dampening, chafing: being the daughter of a post office employee and a pattern cutter doesn't mean she has been cut off from any possible futures, life still being a maze that could lead to the most unexpected places, still dotted with ajar doors that a good kick would open wide. Rabelais – she's read 'Gargantua and Pantagruel', which is more, Beth suspects, than most of the students teeming like beetles along the streets of this university town have done – says: 'Do what thou wilt' and that's exactly what she's going to do, just as it's what she did with that student she took such a shine to; she had done what she wilted and now she's got a sore heart and a question mark cramping her thoughts. She looks over at her boss:

"Maybe there's something on the TV?"

He shrugs.

"Try and find some sport. Punters always like a bit of sport."

She reaches for the remote.

XXX

That Saturday, Delaney — after a long lie-in during which he's observed the ceiling, inch by inch — hasn't felt the need to wash. In fact, now that he's slouching into the adjoining kitchen, he's not sure he can remember the last time he used the bathroom for anything more than to piss and (with increasingly less frequency) to shit. It is early afternoon by the time he slouches into the adjoining kitchen, where Derrick, his young minder, sits at the table, sipping tea.

"A bit too late for breakfast, sir. How about a spot of lunch?"

Delaney runs fingers through his hair then looks at them: their tips are glistening with grease. He looks at Derrick.

"Bread and butter will do, Derrick. Breakfast, lunch, it's all much of a muchness as far as I'm concerned."

"I could do you some pork chops with peas and mashed potato, sir."

"Bread and butter. One slice," says Delaney getting up and — pulling out a plastic-wrapped sliced loaf of white from an enamelled breadbin that might have been new in the 1950s — tugs open the fridge, peers, and takes out a plastic tub of margarine.

"No butter? Has the Service had its budget cut yet again?"

"It's always been margarine, sir."

"Has it? Oh, well..." Delaney smears some on a slice, "...margarine, butter... In fact, Derrick," he stuffs half the slice into his mouth, "I couldn't give a toss."

Crumbs fall onto his T-shirt, down which they slide onto his lap.

"Not too fussy myself, sir."

"Glad to hear it, Derrick, glad to hear it..."

He swallows the rest of the slice.

"...right, that's me done."

He stands up and turns back in the direction of the bedroom.

"Sir."

A hesitant voice.

"What?"

"Spending so much time in bed is bad for your health. You should at least spend a few hours sitting up or standing."

"Is that so?"

"I believe so, sir."

Delaney sighs.

"All right, I'll sit."

He plumps himself down on one of the kitchen's wooden chairs.

"Well, Derrick, what do you suggest we do here? Rummy? Chess? I-Spy?"

"We could watch some television, sir."

"Brilliant! The telly it is, Derrick! What would I do without you?"

Without replying, Derrick gets up and turns it on.

XXXI

I peered at the screen, Ralph and Sarah on either side of me. The fish-eye showed the gentlemen turning in their seats so as to get a good view of the door, where Gibson was now standing:

"Messieurs, the *pièce de résistance!*"

He opened the door and pulled in two small boys by their hands; they were wearing white bath robes. Gibson then stood to one side, leaving them on their own, on display. One was hanging his head, another was shifting uncomfortably on his feet. Sarah, between barely open teeth, said:

"They've been drugged."

Ralph nodded. David's microphone picked up Gibson saying:

"A set of twins, gentlemen..."

"...eight years old today! It's their happy birthday!"

Hayley said:

"Excellent work, Twisty."

Gibson's voice changed to that of a dog trainer:

"Position one!"

Both boys dropped to their knees and inclined their faces to the floor. Gibson flipped up the backs of the birthday twins' bathrobes, exposing their naked behinds.

"I thought we could start by blowing their little candles out."

Out of one pocket of his velvet jacket he removed a pair of colourful birthday cake candles and from the other a Zippo lighter, with whose large flame he lit the little wicks; then, with a magician's flourish, he held one candle up to his audience, bent down slowly, and inserted the unlit end into the first boy's anus. He repeated the operation with his twin brother, then stood up. The candles were now sticking up and out from the twins' behinds, their flames twitching. Some people clapped, but not all, as Sebastian Hayley and Hugh Lowell MP, and my friendly tutor Professor Curtis had all opened their flies and were massaging their penises. David was sitting bolt upright in his chair, his eyes moving from one man to another, his head beginning to shake no. Ralph whispered:

"Not sure how long David's going to hold out. We weren't expecting *this*."

Gibson looked at the men, then gestured to the kneeling boys.

"Who amongst you would like to be first?"

Lowell MP stood up, slowly.

"That'd be me, Ray, if I might."

"Be your guest."

Gibson sat down. Lowell knelt behind the boy, blew out the candle, plucked it out, then leaned forward and sniffed the boy's anus. David shot up. The others' heads turned to him. If

David's mike hadn't been taped not far from his chin, we mightn't have heard him mutter:

"Need the gents."

Sarah tutted.

"He's too early!"

She pointed pointedly at me.

"Off you go! Now!"

In my eagerness I tugged the handle on the van's door in the wrong direction.

"It won't fucking open!"

Ralph slipped off his stool and came over.

"No need to shout."

He turned the handle the right way and one of the two back doors swung open.

"Fast as you can!"

But I was already running, sprinting, feeling the coins jingling in my pocket, aware only of the cold air, the washes of lamppost light and the blur of treed front gardens. When I reached the phone box, glowing yellow at the end of the road, I found an elderly lady in it, nattering away. I rapped several times on one of the miniature panes and shouted the first thing that came into my head:

"I need to call 999, RIGHT NOW! THIS IS AN EMERGENCY!"

Alarmed, she got out of there post-haste and waddled off as fast as she could. I stepped in, fishing out coins and the scrap of paper that Warren had given me and told me not to lose, no matter what. I set up fifty pee in the slot.

"BBC Current Affairs, how can I help you?"

Swallowing down saliva, I said:

"Extension 6661, please."

A short string of clicks were followed by faint strains of 'I'd Like To Teach The World to Sing'.

"Hello?"

"Alexis Skyler?"

"Speaking."

I gave the code word:

"Aretha Franklin."

A pause.

"So what's the address?"

"Twenty-seven Rectory Road, Barnes."

"This *is* serious, right?"

A working-class woman, to go by the accent. I hadn't been aware there were any working-class people working for the BBC, let alone women ones.

"Please come right now. You haven't got much time."

I'd been told to say just that and hang up, but Ms Skyler shoehorned in:

"I've got a full crew on stand-by. If this is a joke, I don't care how fucking underground you are, I'll strangle you all with my own fucking hands."

"Please just *get here!*"

I hung up and pushed the booth door open so hard it swung back into my face. I stepped out and half-walked, half-ran back to the van.

*

By now, Lowell had inserted his penis into the boy's anus and had begun to pump slowly. The boy – who hadn't made a sound until then – gave an audible groan.

David came back into the living-room and sat back down, eyes averted from Lowell and the child. He smoothed down one of his jacket lapels. The signal. Sarah said, slowly:

"He's done it."

Ralph looked at his watch.

"Fourteen and a bit minutes to go. Did you get through to the Beeb, Lou?"

"They're on their way."

On the screen, Curtis stood up, clutching his pre-masturbated penis, went over to where the other twin was still bent over, a still flickering candle in his bottom, and knelt in front of him. Having unzipped his fly, Curtis gripped the boy's head until it was where he wanted it to be. He then leaned down and whispered something we couldn't catch into the boy's ear. The boy's head shifted further forward and began to move back and forth. Curtis watched, transfixed:

"He's a fast learner."

There were a few chuckles but not from Lowell, who, grunting now, was pumping his chosen eight-year-old harder and harder. Then Hayley also got up, took the candle out of the second twin, the one who was fellating Curtis, then removed a little jar of Vaseline from his pocket and smeared it carefully in and around the boy's anus. Then without a word he stuck his penis in, hard, and began pumping in turn.

Ralph and Sarah had turned their heads away, but I could not take my eyes off the specific image of my learned tutor building up to a release of sperm inside a small boy's mouth.

The explosion caught me by surprise.

Curtis, Lowell and Hayley instantaneously tugged their members out of their victims and shot to their feet. The boys themselves swivelled themselves into sitting positions, groggily, eyes frightened wide. Gibson pointed at them:

"Stay where you are!"

Plaster dust was falling from the ceiling, but the room itself had remained intact. Ralph slammed his hand down on the console.

"We got the charge right."

Sarah said:

"Just as well we experimented on those churches."

Curtis glared at Gibson.

"If this is your idea of a joke, Mr Twisty, I don't think much of it."

Gibson snapped:

"Of course it's not a bloody joke!"

Wisps of black smoke had started to creep through the door, which suddenly opened, revealing the man they called Jeeves.

"An explosive device would appear to have gone off in one of the upstairs bedrooms. I suggest the gentlemen leave the premises at once."

Sir Peter Layman, informal intelligence operative, barked:

"It *would* be wise to depart the premises. You go ahead, I'll be out in a jiffy."

He reached into his Gladstone bag and pulled out a cordless phone the size of a loaf of bread.

Sarah leaned into the monitor:

"What's he up to?"

The last words we heard from the room were Gibson's:

"For Christ sake, don't call the police!"

Sarah rapped on the partition that gave onto the front cabin. Warren, who was still sitting there on his own, turned.

"What now?"

"Time you got behind the wheel and drove this thing back to the garage. And time the rest of us got the hell out."

Sarah, Ralph and I jumped out onto the street. Ralph locked the hatch doors and Warren pulled away into Ranelagh Avenue while we wandered over to the Bed and Breakfast, merging into a burgeoning group of local onlookers in which Mavis, Janis, Stevie and Van, back from their recces, had already mingled. Ralph and myself joined them, but not Sarah. I looked around, but couldn't see her. Smoke was billowing out of one of the house's upper windows; a few low, crackling flames were barely visible through the fumes.

A vehicle the size of a double decker bus with the letters BBC painted in white on its black side swerved round the corner of Rectory Road and braked hard just before it reached the crowd; a half-dozen people trotted methodically out laden with cameras, sound mikes and cables. They were followed by a man in a suit with a hand microphone and by a woman who I assumed was Alexis Skyler, the director, given that she immediately began yelling orders:

"Tim, get out there, in front of that fucking house, camera one here, camera two over there. Susy, take the boom to cover Tim."

The technicians and the besuited presenter ran to their positions. Alexis Skyler kept on shouting:

"We've got a live feed, just like the TV crew when the cops took the SLA down in California, so Tim, keep it fucking cool; and cameras, I want clear shots. And GVs of all the fucking rubberneckers…"

The door of the house opened and the men we'd been watching in black and white on a small screen walked out fast in a small scrum, life-sized now and trying hard not to look disconcerted.

"…Christ, we've got ourselves a clutch of fucking VIPs! Tim, get the fuck over to them! Now!"

As the presenter jogged over, with the sound woman and one of the cameramen in tow, the growing audience of neighbours and passers-by gasped and muttered and pointed as it recognised celebrity chef Hayley, then Jumping Jimbo Johnson, then Lowell, MP. But not, of course, Mr Twisty Gibson and professor Curtis and the butler type. Sir Peter Layman came out last, speaking into his electronic loaf. And David? Where the hell was David?

XXXII

Delaney jumps to his feet. On the little screen in front of him are a house on fire, several celebrities being approached by a reporter, the word LIVE flashing red in the top left-hand corner of the screen and the words 'Rectory Road, Barnes, London' flowing across the bottom. The presenter, a mite flustered, turns to the camera:

"We're bringing you this remarkable event live from south London. We do not yet have all the details in hand, but we hope that these gentlemen here will clarify matters…"

A woman's voice off-camera can just be made out:

"GVs! Where are my fucking GVs?"

A cut to another camera shows the group of onlookers and among them are two people Delaney recognises only too well. His short-lived recruit. And that black woman.

Making an effort to sound offhand, Delaney calls out to his minder:

"Derrick, could you be a love and give me a hand with something? I'm in a bit of a fix."

Derrick comes into the room chop-chop.

"Yes, sir?"

Delaney smashes a fist against the side of Derrick's skull, sending him, barely conscious, to the carpet. Delaney strips off

Derrick's jacket, fishes for keys, then uses the jacket's sleeves to tie Derrick's hands behind his back. Then Delaney takes a handkerchief out of his own pocket.

"It's used, I'm afraid, but it'll have to do. Sorry about this. Or perhaps not."

Delaney pulls Derrick's jaw open, stuffs the handkerchief whole into his mouth, unlocks the front door, takes the stairs down three at a time, gets into Derrick's unmarked Ford Escort, and guns the motor.

XXXIII

Television chef Hayley, Lowell the MP and Jimbo Johnson had shielded their silent faces with their hands, as if deep in sudden grief. Peter Layman popped his cordless phone back into his outsize briefcase. Tim the presenter thrust his mike at the man nearest to him.

"What's been going on here?"

Curtis muttered:

"No comment."

"No comment on *what*, sir?"

The six men were now cornered: the onlookers had formed a tightly packed crowd to their left; to their right, the television van had blocked most of the road.

David finally came out of the bed and breakfast, holding the hands of the eight-year-old twins who came to a halt in their white dressing gowns. They had darkish hair, black or brown, cut in uneven pudding bowls that framed freckled, pasty faces, and were looking sluggishly around them. The men from the house were trying to ignore the bystanders, who – as they slowly put two and two together – were growing aggressive. Boos and catcalls alternated with calls for an ambulance for the boys.

"Mr Gibson!"

Sarah had stepped out from the very edge of the crowd to my right – no wonder I hadn't spotted her – and was standing in the middle of the street, both hands closed around a handgun.

Ralph leaned into my ear:

"Walther PDP. Beautiful little piece."

He didn't seem particularly fazed. All the bystanders, however, had suddenly shut up. They and we and the presenter and the crew and David and the twins and all of the men who'd been in the house were staring at her. Especially Gibson aka Mister Twisty, the gun being aimed as it was directly at his chest. She nodded at him.

"Move towards me, slowly."

He did so.

"Stop there."

He was standing on his own now, a few feet away both from us in the crowd and the little group of men and boys.

"Sarah?"

"Hello, Uncle Ray."

"Sarah…"

She raised the barrel until it was in line with his face.

"You piece of shit. You sick bastard."

Stevie, the black woman, called out:

"Alice, that's not what we agreed -"

"This black sheep has been in my sights right from the start and he's going to get what's coming to him. The judges can have the rest of them, lenient though I'm sure they'll be."

Suddenly, she turned her head, her attention caught by the whine of a motor. A brown Mini had manoeuvred its way at speed, two wheels on the pavement and two on the road, through the gap left by the BBC van and was now skidding to a halt smack in front of the B&B. Its doors shot open and two women wearing non-matching denim jeans and jackets jumped out and crouched behind the open car doors, each with two hands clasping guns that were aimed at Sarah.

Ralph whispered:

"Glock 19s."

He seemed fazed now, all right. Alexis Skyler, standing a couple of feet behind the presenter and the rest of the crew, leaned forward to the nearest cameraman:

"I hope you're fucking getting this."

Sir Peter barked at the women from the Mini:

"Took your time!"

"Only one unit on duty today, sir."

He nodded at Sarah:

"Never mind her, just do your job and get me out of here!"

Ex-soldier David, still minding the children, called out to Sarah:

"Alice, these are SRR!"

She kept her gun trained on Gibson. I looked at Ralph:

"SRR?"

"Special Reconnaissance Regiment. They really *are* licensed to -"

"Sarah, stop this, now!"

Stevie had stepped out of the crowd. It was the first time I'd heard anyone in the group forget an alias but I didn't have time to think about that much because I and Ralph and several other bystanders were shoved to one side by a bearded man in crumpled black clothes who had made a bedraggled beeline for Stevie and now slammed her face hard with the palm of his hand.

"You lying bitch!"

Sarah swung round to train her gun on him:

"Stay away from her!"

I was keeping my eyes on the women in denim, their weapons still trained on Sarah, but they were holding their fire. Sarah swivelled her aim away from Gibson and fired. The bearded man who had hit Stevie tipped over, yelling and clutching his ankle. Only then did I recognise James Delaney, my erstwhile handler. When I looked back at the street, Sarah had dropped her gun and was sprinting towards the gap left by the TV van. The SSR women lowered and holstered their weapons. I felt a tap on the shoulder.

"Get out of here now. Don't follow us."

Ralph. I looked round but he'd gone. As had the others.

Sir Peter Layman pointed at the anchorman:

"Stop the cameras! Right this instant!"

From her spot just behind the crew, Skyler yelled:

"Keep fucking filming!"

One of two SSR operatives stood up and opened one of the rear doors.

"Step into the vehicle, sir!"

Layman scuttled over to the waiting backseat, buttoning his yawning fly as best he could. The women slipped into the front and the Mini pulled away fast.

It had barely done so when a convoy of two ambulances, a panda car, a police holding van, a fire engine and a tender truck – their sirens whooping, their rotating lights flashing – now hurtled up Rectory Road from the left and came to a halt, the bed and breakfast to their left, the crowd to their right, the TV van straight ahead of them. The bystanders and myself stepped back onto the pavement, leaving Delaney on the road, clutching his ankle. Two ambulance men raised him onto a gurney, and two concerned looking nurses went over to the dressing-gowned boys and talked to David for a moment before leading the twins over to the second ambulance. The other men who'd been in the house, their jackets now pulled over their heads, were being helped into the holding van by the policemen from the panda car. The firemen had begun to unreel hoses, eyes on the little that was left of the smoke and fire in the upper floor of the B&B. Alexis Skyler yelled:

"Get the fucking celebs, Tim!"

But the black maria's doors had already been slammed shut and it was starting to move back up Rectory Road, followed by the panda car,.

I looked over at where David had been standing in front of the B&B. He too had vanished.

Another car was now pulling up from my left: an unmarked Ford Escort with a flashing blue light stuck onto its roof. Two plainclothes police got out, wearing beige overcoats, and began looking purposefully around for, I had no doubt, members of The Vanguard.

I edged my way over to the edge of the crowd, trying not to look like I was in a hurry, and as soon as I was out of the throng, started to walk at a pace faster than I'd intended in the direction of Putney Common. Behind me a man who I had no doubt was wearing a beige overcoat yelled:

"You, stop there!"

I broke into a run and quickly made it across Ranelagh Avenue and onto the common and then along a narrow path, into the darkness of a nearby clump of trees. The becoated men had stopped shouting, but I could hear the tamping of their soles on the path behind me. I felt my lungs hurting as I scarpered out of the trees and across a clearing and onto the pavement of a main road. Out of breath, my chest was now making little helpless grabs for air when a expensive looking car so quiet it might have been an outsize moving cushion drove up and stopped in front of me; the back door swung open and a woman's voice I hadn't heard in what felt like ages called out:

"Get in!"

I jumped into the back, hearing the door clunk shut behind me and locks clicking into place, smelling leather, feeling some g-force as the car pulled away at speed. Through the rear window, I could see my pursuers had reached the kerb but were already looking very small indeed. The driver, without turning, said:

"Bentley T-series. Nice little motor."

I'd heard that voice before too, but couldn't place it and besides, I was more interested in the first one. Beth said:

"Hello, you."

She leaned forward and pecked me on the lips. As buildings darted past, she explained how she'd tried to find me by getting in touch with Ralph's father – she pointed at the driver, who raised his hand by way of a hello – who had at first given her the brush-off – he grunted a laugh – but when she saw both me and Ralph and Sarah on TV this evening she decided to get in touch with him again and this time he didn't hesitate, picking her up then racing up to Barnes, her looking up Rectory

Road - named on the TV news broadcast - in his A to Z. They were driving along Mill Hill Road when they spotted me rushing out of the common, a hundred or so yards ahead of them.

We were now heading south.

"What about Ralph?"

His father checked the rear-view before turning onto the M3.

"Ralph'll be fine," he said, "as will Sarah. And all the others, for that matter."

"He knew everything," Beth said, "right from the start. The formation of the group, the strategy. Everything, except their plans for the house on Rectory: that was top secret."

A small chuckle from the head in front of me.

"Should have known Ralph and Sarah weren't going to tell me *everything*."

"Where are we going?"

"Got the passport they gave you?"

I checked my inside pocket. Van's forgery was still there.

"Yes."

"As for Beth, she doesn't need a new one, there's no one after *her*."

We reached Portsmouth in a couple of hours.

EPILOGUE

Warren had calculated it would take him a week to get the sounds and images recorded in the van to all the media: not only the major radio and TV broadcasters but also the regional ones, and the national papers plus the local ones. Plus *Private Eye*.

Beth and I took a week to reach Montpellier from Cherbourg via a roundabout route, changing trains and coaches frequently.

The day we arrived, we moved into a small furnished flat on the outskirts of Montpellier, thanks to the cash Ralph's Dad had supplied us with. Beth called him as soon as we got there, using an agreed code:

"Hi there, Eve here."

"Eve! It's been a while!"

"How are all your cats and dogs doing?"

"Just fine. Sleeping like logs."

"That's good to hear. And what about the canaries?"

"Well that's the odd thing. Not one of them has started singing. Not even the one with the bad eye."

"And the budgie you got a week ago?"

"I've lost the bugger. Not a clue as to its whereabouts."

"What a pity. Well, nice talking to you."

"'Bye, Eve. Sorry I can't be more positive."

In other words, none of the members of the Vanguard had been caught, none of the material distributed by Warren had appeared anywhere, *Private Eye* included, and the live footage taken by Alexis Skyler outside the Oakhill Bed & Breakfast – which had only shown viewers a brief shot of a few well-known faces, without offering any commentary – had never been shown or mentioned again. Anywhere.

Unable to do a thing about this silence under which the results of so much planning and risk-taking had been buried so deep, we decided to wait and see if there were any further developments. Beth's French, I wasn't too surprised to find out, was better than mine. She found a job as a waitress in quite a smart restaurant and I landed a job as a busboy in the same establishment.

Montpellier being a large city with plenty of tourists, its newsagents stocked foreign newspapers. We'd been living there for almost two months when a Saturday stroll in the Parc Rimbaud took us past a large kiosk one of whose racks was loaded with British tabloids and broadsheets, every headline of which was reporting the death of Hugh Lowell, MP.

He had been found slumped in an armchair at home, an empty bottle of barbiturates on the floor. The police had found no sounds of breaking and entering, nor any signs of a struggle. Lowell, they concluded, had died alone, by his own hand.

We decided to start checking the English papers more often, which was how we found out that six weeks later, Jumping Jimbo Johnson had accidentally fallen off a cliff near his second home in Devon. His blood alcohol level was high enough, according to a doctor interviewed by one of the papers, to have induced a total blackout.

Three whole months went by before the multilingual chef Sebastian Hayley drowned in a Venice canal while walking off a large dinner. The Italian authorities concluded that he had slipped on the seaweed – traces of which had been found on one of his shoes – that was plentiful at the water's edge along many of the canals. At the press conference after the autopsy, the police spokesman gave a little shrug:

"Non è la primera volta que succede."

At first, Beth and I weren't sure what to make of all this, not least because the back stories which soon appeared after these three well-known people's deaths seemed likely enough: Lowell, it turned out, had had a history of depression; Jim Johnson had had a serious drink problem, which only a few close friends had known about; and as for Hayley, it turned out that tourists in Venice frequently slipped on the canal-side seaweed: he just happened to be one of the few who didn't know how to swim.

And yet…

Half a year later, we received an anonymous telegram from Brussels: 'Today's Times. Obituaries.' In the copy we bought, the name, birth and death dates, and a potted summary of his life – ended the day before by a cardiac arrest – was all the information provided about the demise of professor Alan Curtis of Wellingford University's Wolverton College.

Eight months after Curtis's death, Sir Peter Layman – being as he once had been a top-tier civil servant – was accorded a quarter of a page in the broadsheets after he was fatally injured in a car accident in a remote, rainswept corner of Scotland.

It was only then that Beth said:

"I think they could be killing them."

"*What?*"

"Ever so carefully, one after the other."

My jury was still out. Suicides, accidents, overdoses and heart attacks were things that happened, after all, and happened quite often.

"That may be so," said Beth, "but I still wouldn't like to be in the shoes of the one that's left, whatshisname, the fixer."

"Raymond Gibson," I said, remembering Sarah aiming at her uncle.

As if on cue, Mr Gibson appeared in the papers just a couple of days after Layman: abducted in a wood outside Wells, he'd been tied up, shot in the head and chest and left in a roadside ditch with several photographs of the faces of small boys and girls scattered over his corpse. The ammunition used had come from two different shotguns, and I for one had no doubt that one of them was Finnish and the other, a Blaser twelve gauge.

"Well," said Beth, "was my hunch right or was it right?"

Without a shadow of a doubt. My jury came to the conclusion that the Vanguard was guilty on all counts. I imagined them taking on each person on in pairs, each couple skilfully disguised by South Asian Janis, the former make-up girl. She and head-scarfed Mavis had dealt with Johnson and Hayley, perhaps; and ex-soldier David and Irish Warren with Sir Peter and possibly professor Curtis; Van and Stevie with Lowell MP, maybe. Sarah and Ralph with Gibson, for sure. Only 'Jeeves' appeared to have got away. Or maybe not.

All along, I realised, this must have been their plan C, should all else fail. And it didn't surprise me one bit that they hadn't told me about it. On the contrary – I thought, as I bit into a chocolate croissant, sending a few of its crumbs down onto the newspaper photo of Gibson's still face, a black hole in its forehead – they were right not to: I would have balked at murder. But, I realised with some astonishment, I was very glad indeed that the others hadn't. Indeed, it even struck me that the deaths of their victims had helped make the world a slightly better place. As I went on sipping my coffee and chewing my croissant, sending yet more flakes of crust onto Gibson's face, I felt an unfamiliar warmth well up in my gut and spread into my chest from where it oozed pleasantly up into my head. I glanced at Beth, who was reading the same news about Gibson in a different paper, seated opposite me, there on the half-sunny terrace of the Coffee Club Montpellier, whose furniture was now glowing, whose light was now filled with tiny sparkles.

"You've got the day off, right?"

She looked up.

"You too. Right?"

"Let's do something special. Something we've never done before."

She shrugged.

"Like what?"

That stymied me for an instant.

"I don't know and I don't care. Something different. Anything different!"

She came up with a really, really good idea.

Banyoles/Barcelona, 2019-2023

Among the books that helped provide material for this novel are:

BRYAN, John, *'This Soldier Still At War: True Story of Joe Remiro and the Symbionese Liberation Army'*, London, Quartet Books, 1974.

DALY, Anthony, *'Playland: Secrets of a Forgotten Scandal'*, London, Mirror books, 2018.

DANZCUK, Simon, *'Smile For The Camera: The Double Life of Cyril Smith'*, London, Biteback Publishing, 2015.

DAVIES, DAN, *'In Plain Sight: The Life and Lies of Jimmy Savile'*, London, Quercus, 2015.

DEAKIN, Michael and WILLIS, John, *'Johnny Go Home'*, London, Futura Publications, 1976.

HEARST, Patricia Campbell, *'Every Secret Thing'*, New York, Doublday, 1981.

TOOBIN, Jeffrey, *'American Heiress: The Kidnapping, Crimes and Trial of Patty Hearst'*, London, Profile Books, 2017.